THE SECOND
CORONA BOOK OF
HORROR
STORIES

THE SECOND CORONA BOOK OF
HORROR STORIES

edited by
LEWIS WILLIAMS

First published in the United Kingdom in 2018

by Corona Books UK
www.coronabooks.com

ISBN 978-1-9996579-2-5

Cover design by Martin Bushell
www.creatusadvertising.co.uk

CONTENTS

INTRODUCTION

Welcome to *The Second Corona Book of Horror Stories.* We've put our hearts and souls into this project, and, I think it's safe to say, the authors herein have put their blackest hearts and darkest souls into their contributions.

We've assembled this collection with the help of a worldwide call for submissions, to which we had a fantastic response. We certainly received a lot more stories that we really liked and wanted to include than we had room for in the book. In fact, this book was always intended to, like the original *Corona Book of Horror Stories*, include 16 stories, but it has 17 because we couldn't bear to exclude any of the stories you'll find here. You won't find star names here, but you will find genuinely brilliant writing talent. That's what this book is all about and what we're all about, taking the time and trouble to seek out and celebrate the talent out there that mainstream publishers are apt to ignore. Perhaps some of this is because they're a bit sniffy about horror, a genre that seems to get increasingly sidelined by some. We, on the other hand, love horror. And it is a field in which great writing is more than possible, as the stories here prove.

I don't want to go into any great detail here about any of the stories as it's better you read them for yourself. Suffice it to say that you will find variety: supernatural horror and natural (all too human) horror, different points of view and new takes in fresh lights on traditional horror themes.

The Second Corona Book of Horror Stories is also a truly transatlantic affair. However you count it, roughly half the stories are from American or Canadian authors and half from British authors. I say 'however you count it' as we have one American author and one Canadian author who have chosen to make the UK their home (American Wondra Vanian, who lives in Wales, and Canadian Suzan St Maur, who has made England her home). Those two aside, we've chosen to keep the stories by North American authors with their native spelling. Elsewhere this book is presented in British English (where we have colours, sceptics and centres rather than colors, skeptics and centers etc.) Although it's sometimes quite subtle, the differences extend to punctuation too, and we've respected the fact that Americans favour the use of double quotes for speech, whereas we Brits, it seems, prefer single quotes when it comes to fiction in print.

If you're thinking, by the way, that the English-speaking/reading world isn't only Britain and North America, then of course you're right, and if you're a writer of horror from elsewhere, then we want to hear from you for our next collection. Follow @CoronaBooksUK and look out for our next call for submissions!

In the meantime, there's just a couple of final things for me to say before we get on with the show. Firstly, if you enjoy this book, do be sure to check out the original

Corona Book of Horror Stories as well. You'll find other stories by some of the authors in this book there, as well as a healthy dose of great stories by other writers too. Secondly, especially if you enjoyed particular stories, do be sure to check out the author websites and Twitter accounts listed at the end of the book. All of the authors will welcome website visits and you following them on Twitter, and you'll be rewarded with some other great writing. I said earlier that there were no authors who are star names in this book; I should have said *yet*. There's so much talent here that I'm sure at least one of the authors in this book will go on to achieve major prominence.

Now, on with the (horror) show!

Lewis Williams

MR CRUEL

Phillip Drake

Billy Craven sat at the dining room table, his legs swinging back and forth like a pendulum on a clock as he deftly guided the black felt tip pen on the piece of paper in front of him.

'That's an interesting picture, Billy. What is it?' The question came from his babysitter Elaine who had sidled up to him without Billy noticing. As she asked her question, she turned her head to one side then the other as if changing her viewing angle would give her a better perspective.

'It's a man,' Billy replied, the pen in his right hand not leaving the page as he glanced upwards.

Elaine bent over slightly to get a closer look and placed a hand on Billy's left shoulder. 'And does this man have a name?'

Billy nodded. 'Mr Cruel,' he said, as he dropped the black felt tip and reached for a red one.

'Is he somebody you know?' Elaine asked. Something about the figure Billy had drawn bothered her.

Billy had so far drawn the man in nothing other than black, the face half hidden beneath the wide brim of a hat, his arms and legs longer than they should be; but now he drew the hands in red, blood red, and dabbed the red pen from the hands down to the feet, like drips.

Elaine felt a sudden coldness creep over her skin.

'I see him sometimes,' Billy said whilst snapping the lid of the red felt tip back in place with a satisfying click. 'I was frightened at first, but now I'm okay. I think he likes me.' Billy's emotionless delivery seemed to give his words a somewhat baleful edge.

Elaine regarded him curiously. 'Where do you see him, Billy?'

'Sometimes at night when I look out of my bedroom window.' Billy's reply carried no trace of worry, and he began to add the letters that spelt out Mr Cruel above the head of the sinister-looking figure. 'And sometimes he's in my room when I wake up.'

'In... in your room?' Elaine could feel the fine, wispy hairs on the back of her neck rise up.

'Yes, he's never hurt me though, although he does do bad things – that's why I call him Mr Cruel.'

'Have you told your mum about this?' Elaine was by now beginning to feel that she should have turned down this particular babysitting assignment.

'The thing is, my mum thinks I do these bad things when really it's Mr Cruel's fault,' Billy replied. He'd almost put all the pens away when he suddenly pulled out the black felt tip and began drawing again.

'What bad things does your mum blame you for?' Elaine asked, beads of sweat forming on her brow.

Billy gave a little shrug of his shoulders. 'Just stuff.'

'What kind of stuff?'

'The cat died and she blamed me.'

Elaine detected a hint of sadness in Billy's voice, or was it regret? 'How did the cat die?' she asked quietly.

'I don't know,' replied Billy, his right hand busy on the paper once more. 'Mum wouldn't tell me, but that night when I saw Mr Cruel, he had blood on his hands.'

Before Elaine could elicit more information, the baby monitor, which she had earlier placed on the coffee table, sparked into life with the sound of infant cries.

'That'll be your sister,' Elaine sighed. 'I'd better go and see what's up,' she said as she made to walk towards the stairs.

'Mr Cruel doesn't like my sister either,' Billy said, his words halting his babysitter mid-stride.

'What did you say?' Elaine found that the words were almost sticking in the dryness of her throat as she spun round to face him.

'He doesn't like her, just like he didn't like the cat,' Billy replied. He was still working on his picture and his face was one of emotionless concentration. 'And he doesn't like you either.'

Elaine walked back towards Billy, his last statement drowned out by the noise coming from the baby monitor, its arc of LED lights moving from green to red as the intensity of the little girl's cries increased.

'What are you drawing now?' Elaine asked, but Billy put his left arm over the paper, spoiling her view.

'Wait till I've finished,' Billy snapped.

'Okay, okay. I'm going to see to your sister, then I think I'd better phone your mother.'

Billy said nothing; he just carried on with his drawing.

* * *

It didn't take Elaine long to sooth Billy's baby sister. After changing her nappy, she carried the infant over to the rocking chair, the one that afforded views of the back garden from the nursery's window, and rocked her back to sleep. The moonlight cast long shadows across the room through the gap in the curtains as Elaine hummed a nursery rhyme.

It took only a few minutes for Elaine to be confident enough to put the little girl back in her cot, although she hung around for a little while just in case the baby stirred once more.

Sitting back in the chair, Elaine fished out her mobile phone from her jeans pocket, scrolled through the contacts and upon finding the children's mother pressed the call button.

Billy's mum answered on the third ring.

'Hi Julie, it's Elaine. How's the exhibition going?' She thought it best not to dive straight in with her concerns about Billy's artwork.

'Fine thanks, Elaine. How are the kids? There's nothing wrong, is there?' Elaine could barely hear Julie's voice above the background chatter.

'Well... er... kind of. I've just changed the baby's nappy and put her back to sleep, but I want to ask you something about Billy.' Elaine hoped that her apprehension didn't convey itself in her voice.

'Did you say Billy?' Julie asked, and Elaine could hear her shushing someone. 'I'm sorry, Elaine, it's quite noisy where I am. I'll move somewhere quieter.' There was a pause, and Elaine could hear a door slam and the background din all but disappeared.

'Sorry about that,' Julie said, and for the first time Elaine noticed that Julie was slurring her words a little.

'So, what about Billy? What's he been up to now?'

'It's nothing serious,' Elaine began – and in her mind she hoped she was right about that – 'it's just that he was drawing this figure, and when I asked him about it he started saying some strange things.'

'Let me guess, Mr Cruel?' Julie replied.

'Er… yeah… You know about that?' Elaine asked as she glanced out of the window.

'Yes, I know all about it. Look, I'll be honest, I've been having a few problems with Billy lately.'

'What kind of problems?'

'It's nothing to worry about—' Julie began to reply and then broke off to tell someone that she was on the phone and could they keep the noise down. Elaine heard distant laughter in the background. 'He's just been playing up a bit that's all,' Julie continued, 'and blaming it on this Mr Cruel character.'

'Billy seems to think that Mr Cruel is real.' Elaine didn't realise it, but she was almost whispering her words now.

'He's just got a good imagination that's all, like his mother.' Julie laughed slightly.

'Yeah, I guess so,' Elaine replied, her words not sounding convincing to her own ears.

'Look, if he gives you any major problems, give his dad a ring. He's closer to home than I am. The number's on the fridge,' Julie replied, and no sooner had she finished speaking than the background noise rose once again. 'Look, Elaine, I have to go; I'm wanted. I'll be home first thing in the morning, and don't forget, Billy goes to bed at nine on the dot, no exceptions.' With that, Julie said goodbye and ended the call.

Elaine moved the phone from her ear and stared at the screen for a few seconds, unsure of what to do next. The time was just past half-past eight, and she thought that maybe now would be a good time to get Billy ready for bed, as once the boy was asleep he couldn't get up to any mischief.

As Elaine was about to stand up, a noise coming from the direction of the cot caused her to pause. At first, she thought the baby had stirred, but when she listened more keenly she heard that the noise was coming from the baby monitor.

Billy was talking.

This was strange. In order for her to hear him, Elaine came to realise, he had to be holding down the talk button on the parent unit of the baby monitor, which was designed for parents to soothe their baby's cries by talking to them remotely. Whatever Billy was saying, it seemed he wanted her to hear it.

Billy's words were distant, though, as if he weren't holding the unit close enough to his mouth. She could make out snatches of one side, his side, of an apparent conversation. 'She's upstairs with my sister... No, I don't think so... In the kitchen... But I like her.'

At that last remark, she broke her silence and hissed into the baby monitor unit by the cot, 'Billy, who are you talking to?' There was a tremor in her voice that she couldn't hide.

There was no reply from the boy.

'Billy, answer me, is there someone down there with you?'

No reply, just a gentle hiss of white noise.

The quietness was unnerving, and Elaine's mind raced with the options she had open to her. She could call the police, but that might be an overreaction. She could call Julie back, but there was no guarantee she would be in any fit state to do anything, even if she did answer the phone. That left calling Billy's father, but that raised its own problems. Julie said his number was on the fridge, which meant that Elaine would have no option but to go downstairs. Also, she'd never even spoken to Billy's dad; how would she explain calling him out of the blue, let alone saying that Billy might be in danger, or worse *be* the danger.

Elaine opened the nursery door wider and peered out. The hallway was empty, as she expected it to be. The silence was eerie as if she were the only one in the house, but of course she wasn't. She looked back over her shoulder at the baby sleeping soundly in the cot. A faint reassuring smile showed at the corners of the child's mouth.

She made her way along the landing. A lassitude in her step and a muzziness in her head made clear thinking difficult.

Reaching the top of the stairs, she took a couple of deep breaths, tapped the phone in her jeans pocket for reassurance, and proceeded to descend the stairs that led to the living room. She descended slowly, disturbed and anxious about the unnatural silence around her.

When she was halfway down, Elaine peered over the bannister rail into the living room. Billy's drawing things were still on the table, but there was no sign of him.

She called his name, tentatively at first, then with more authority on the second calling.

No answer.

Stepping off the last step, she made for the table and the piece of paper there that seemed to be beckoning her to look at it. As she got nearer, it looked as though the paper might be blank after all, but the relief that thought bought her was short-lived. She could see the faint lines through the paper. The page was face down.

'Billy, where are you? Are you in the kitchen?' she called out as she slowly moved her right hand towards the drawing. Still no answer. 'Stop messing about, this isn't funny.' In one quick motion, she grabbed the piece of paper from the table and turned it over.

When she had left Billy to see to his sister there had only been one figure on the page; now there were two, and the new figure was lying at the feet of the figure of Mr Cruel that he had drawn earlier. It didn't take Elaine long to realise that this second figure was meant to be her.

The figure was wearing jeans and a pink top, as she did, and had blonde hair; but it also had one additional thing that she didn't. Something was sticking out of the chest of the female figure, and no matter how much Elaine tried to think of what else it could be, her mind would return to her original conclusion. It was a knife or some other sharp object.

Elaine felt her skin crawl at the sight of it. She swallowed hard to keep the bile from reaching her mouth.

Tentatively, Elaine made for the kitchen door, but stopped once she was within reach of the handle. She stared at the handle as if fearing to touch it. Eventually, she reached for it. It felt as though its coldness were leaping along her hand to her wrist, the sensation intensified by the clamminess of her own skin.

'Billy, I'm warning you, stop this now. You're not scaring me.' Elaine's voice was croaky, and she wondered who she was trying to convince that she wasn't frightened, Billy or herself.

Taking several deep breaths to steel herself, she pulled the door open. The first thing she saw was Billy standing by the sink at the far end of the kitchen. He had his back to her.

'Billy, what's wrong? What are you doing?'

'I don't want to look,' Billy said, his words coming out between sniffs, and Elaine realised he must have been crying.

'What have you done?'

'Nothing… but Mr Cruel will.' Billy's words were almost lost in between sobs.

'Look Billy…' Elaine struggled to keep her voice calm. She took a couple of steps further into the kitchen. 'You need to stop with this Mr Cruel thing. He doesn't exist; he's just someone you blame for when you do something bad.'

Billy's sobs grew louder, but he said nothing.

* * *

Back in the living room, the piece of paper on the table began to move, slowly at first and then more violently, lifting off the table slightly as if caught in a brisk draught. But it wasn't just the paper that moved; one of Billy's drawings seemed to be changing, morphing into something else, something solid.

The paper started to bend, to crumple and crease as Elaine continued to quiz Billy in the kitchen, unaware of what was happening behind her. A solitary finger emerged from the paper, the skin gnarled like the bark on an ancient tree, the long yellow nails cracked and brittle.

It was quickly joined by two more, then the hand, then a wrist showing the cuff of an old and frayed shirt. Further to the right, another hand began to emerge, and soon two forearms reached upwards out of the paper like tentacles.

When the elbows emerged the arms bent, the hands resting on the table for purchase as a black fedora hat broke the surface of the paper.

* * *

'You turned the paper over, didn't you?' Billy's question took Elaine by surprise and she stiffened.

'I wanted to look at your drawing,' she stammered, iciness crawling over her skin as she spoke.

'You shouldn't have done that.' Billy turned his head slightly to the right, and for a second Elaine thought he was going to turn to face her. He didn't, but she could see the tears glinting on his cheek.

'Why not?' Elaine asked, but as Billy turned back to stare at the wall, she heard a noise behind her. Her first thought was that it was the baby monitor sparking into life once more, so she ignored it and pressed on. 'Billy, answer me.' Her voice was heavy with frustration and a rising anger.

Billy said nothing, but started crying again, more than before, huge hearty sobs of despair.

'Billy, why don't you—' Elaine's sentence was cut short by the sudden realisation that there *was* someone behind her. Whirling around, she found herself looking up at the figure of a man dressed in an old and creased black suit, a discoloured white shirt peeping out from beneath the jacket. His eyes were hidden beneath the shadow cast by the wide brim of his hat, but even so

Elaine sensed a red glow somewhere beyond the darkness. His skin was a milky white colour, and there was an accompanying aroma of staleness, like damp socks drying on a radiator.

Billy stayed where he was, his body convulsing slightly with each sob, and as he heard Elaine scream a warm trickle ran down his right leg and pooled at his feet.

The scream ended abruptly, cut off before it could reach maximum pitch; and as a streak of warm blood splattered the back of Billy's T-shirt, he muttered one sentence to himself, 'I bet I get blamed for this.'

BACK TO THE SOIL

Tina Grehm

P he felt hot tears drip onto her bare shoulder followed by the precise edge of a blade pressing against her skin, just under her throat.

She swallowed hard. She knew this was coming and though she should have been afraid a wave of relief washed over her. She opened her eyes slowly, focusing on the woman above her.

Karen was straddling her waist, leaning over her, and Phe couldn't help admiring the other woman. She was maybe in her mid-thirties, but Phe couldn't be sure. They'd never discussed it. They'd never had reason to.

However old she was, there weren't many wrinkles on Karen's skin. No laugh lines, no crow's feet, not even the beginning of them. Probably because of how hard it was to make Karen smile at first. Less so in the past few months, but they hadn't had enough time together for Phe to leave lines on that pretty face.

The thin comforter they were snuggled under the night before was now all but gone, bunched around Karen's bare waist, leaving them both half-exposed.

Golden afternoon light was dimmed by sheer red curtains that cast the room in a crimson glow, a glow that wasn't enough to reach Karen's face through the veil that her hair made as it hung around her hunched shoulders.

Beautiful, Phe found herself thinking. Her chest tightened uncomfortably, leaving her breathless at the sight. Utterly beautiful. She had never loved someone as much as she loved Karen. She'd never felt so understood, so completely loved in return.

And now they were here.

Karen's eyes were red from crying – she could see that much at least – and she wondered how long Karen had been awake laboring over what she was about to do. Had Karen even slept the night before? Phe could imagine her lying there, staring up at the ceiling and quietly mourning before finally getting the courage to get out of bed and get the knife. Phe was a notoriously heavy sleeper; and whenever Karen left the bed, she wasn't woken at all. She slept like the—

"I don't want you to go," Karen choked out.

"I know," Phe replied.

Phe didn't know what else to say. She couldn't stay. They both knew that. She pressed up against the razor edge of the blade, felt it break the skin, but she didn't feel any pain, not until the nick started to bleed. Even then, it caused nothing more than a dull throb and ache that felt like want. She wished she could tell Karen that she wouldn't leave, that this didn't have to happen, but even if she gave voice to the idea, they'd both know it wasn't true. This is exactly what had to happen.

Phe couldn't remain there, trapped in rotting flesh, and Karen was the one to free her.

They both knew it had to be her, Karen, here and, apparently, now. From the beginning Karen was to be her own angel of mercy, the one who would break the chains that tethered her to this cage of meat and bone. This wasn't a surprise to either of them, but that didn't make it any easier.

"It's alright." Phe could see that Karen's gaze was fixed on the trickle of blood starting to trace its way along her clavicle. For a woman used to dealing with cadavers, Karen was suddenly so hesitant. Maybe because those bodies didn't look alive, because they didn't speak and move and touch. They didn't kiss her and tell her how they loved her.

"They are just meat. Empty," Karen had told her that first time in the morgue. Karen was working alone that night, which meant no one would be around to interrupt. "Are you sure you want to watch this?" Karen finally asked, shooting Phe an uncertain look.

Phe had nodded mutely, her gaze caught on the scalpel in Karen's hand as it was poised over the still chest of the corpse on the table. She watched the fine edge of the knife descend and envied the practiced way in which Karen used it. Its handle had felt the caress of Karen's fingers so often, had been used like an extension of those slender arms, had been allowed an intimacy that Phe so craved, and she felt, for a moment, jealous of it.

It was then that Phe knew she was in love.

"Phe?" A pause and then, "Phoenix?"

Phe had been so enraptured by the glint of steel in the too-bright fluorescent lights she had missed the way the scalpel had carved open a large Y across the chest of the cadaver and down the abdomen.

"I'm watching," she had replied, giving a nod that told Karen to keep going.

Rubbery flesh came apart at the edges and Karen's fingers pressed into the folds, making Phe's tongue dart out and swipe across her suddenly too dry lips. Phe imagined she was on that cold slab, Karen's fingers pushing into *her* body, peeling a thick layer of meat away to expose everything inside. The flesh fell away so easily once it'd been cut, all of it, together, looking like the layers of the earth Phe so itched to be buried under.

Subsoil, regolith, and bedrock, the foundations for thick, pale roots that branched out in rich dirt.

Skin, fat, and muscle interlaced with bright blue veins that once pumped blood through a now still heart.

Phe didn't breathe until her body remembered it had to. She still didn't know why; dead women didn't need air. She tried to avoid the thought. Confronting the details of her death – or illusion of living – caused panic to rise up in her throat, burning like bile and making her dizzy. She preferred to not question her state of being. It was easier that way.

Her state of being. The reminder drew her back to where she lay, Karen above her, poised to kill. She wondered if she would be taken apart like that, if Karen would want to explore her as intimately as those bodies in the morgue. She hoped so. There was something about the idea of someone else taking such care with her and being inside of this body, elbow deep inside of it, touching all of the nooks and crannies that had been hidden from the world.

They were both still, the rumbling of cars and muffled chatter of pedestrians outside the apartment window the only sound, aside from Karen's occasional sniff and her heavy breathing. Through the paper-thin walls of the apartment they could hear a neighbor click on a TV, flicking through channels before settling on some horror flick. The audio pushed through the cheap plaster and drywall, bringing to their ears the muffled screams of a woman being killed and the grating high whine of violins followed by bone cracking and the soppy wet sound of flesh tearing.

Phe felt Karen shake suddenly, violently, then pull back.

The blade was lifted high, brought down in a quick arc. Phe expected a sharp pain, prepared herself for it, though she didn't flinch. Her eyes never left Karen's wet cheeks and furrowed brows and flushed skin.

The knife jammed into the mattress by Phe's head and disappointment bloomed in her chest.

Not yet, but soon. Karen just needed time, needed to prepare herself a little more.

"I'm sorry. God, Phe, I'm so sorry. I can't. I can't yet." Karen began to sob, her head falling forward as her shoulders shook. She lifted a hand to her mouth to stifle the despondent moan that tried to bubble up from her throat.

Phe felt tears prick the corners of her own eyes and she tried not to let herself cry too. She didn't want Karen to think she was upset. Things were hard enough as it was.

"It's okay. It's alright, baby. Shhh." Phe's hands lifted to rub Karen's arms, to slide along freckled skin, tracing the curves and hard lines of the bone that she could almost feel beneath. She cooed sweet nothings until Karen's sobs turned into light hiccups and the other woman settled down next to her in bed again, face pressed into her shoulder and brown hair fanning across Phe's chest.

She wondered if Karen were sleeping, but after a moment fingers found her hand to ghost over the lines on her palm. Not sleeping just despondent.

"I'm sorry," Karen murmured again, sounding tired.

Phe pressed a kiss to Karen's forehead. "I can wait."

They lapsed into silence again, neither of them knowing what to say.

Phe closed her eyes, imagining the smell of earth instead of the lavender scent of Karen's shampoo that filled her nose now. She imagined how it would feel to become a part of it, how her body would bloat and then begin to decay, becoming a host for maggots and nightcrawlers. She could almost feel them worming their way under her humid dead flesh, flesh that, as time wore on, would rot away until there were nothing but skeletal remains. Eventually, given a decade or so, that too would crack and crumble until it was absorbed into the soil.

It was all she could dream about in these quiet moments, ever since she'd woken up in the hospital a dead woman.

Having a heart valve replaced was risky, sure, but the risk was low these days. She was supposed to be healed and made whole and new. She hadn't been. The doctors told her she was healthy, and the heart monitor she'd spent nearly a month hooked up to attested to that, but she knew she hadn't made it out of the operating room. She'd lain in that hospital trying to heal after her surgery and knew it was useless to try. She was encumbered by failing flesh.

It was at the hospital that she'd met Karen.

She'd been forcing herself to eat and would take walks at various times, because the doctors said she should, that it'd help her heal and get back into the real world, and because she hadn't told them there was no point. They bothered her often, fussing over how much weight she was losing, how she was sleeping all the time, how she wasn't responsive when her family came to visit.

She wanted to be left alone, wanted to let herself waste away quietly and peacefully, but that wouldn't be allowed to happen here.

The certainty of that was enough to have her trying to feign interest in regaining her health.

She'd force herself out of bed and shuffle into the hall.

"Going for a walk," she'd assure the nurse, who would smile at her and give a little nod.

She wouldn't have any destination in mind, but she'd always end up in the same place, in the quiet basement, always walking down the same antiseptic-smelling halls with sickly green walls on either side of her. The door at the end always had light spilling out from beneath it, even when it was very late at night. There was no marker on it aside from the room number, but Phe knew it was where she needed to be. The sense of belonging there, of being a part of whatever was in that room behind that closed door, was a desperate gnawing feeling that stayed with her during the day, haunted her when she slept, and had her pressing on during her walks, always coming back despite how hesitant she was to actually enter.

She had come night after night, lingering outside until fatigue dragged her back to her room and into bed.

She remembered the moment she had finally decided to get up the courage to go in. Outside the door, she'd rested her head against the polished yellow wood and gripped her fingers around the door knob. Still, she hesitated to push it open. It seemed like she was making a choice, some decision she couldn't come back from, and that gave her pause. Is this what she wanted? She didn't know what *this* was or could mean, but if it were a way out of this hell she'd woken up in, then she wanted it. She rubbed her thumb over the smooth metal knob, considered letting go, then turned it.

And there Karen was, backlit by harsh bright lights and against a solid white backdrop. She was bent over a body. Blood stained her smock, coated her gloved hands, and painted her sleeves all the way up to her elbows. Music was playing somewhere in the room, filling the spaces with an eerie wailing voice that said lovers could grow old together, that each day could be lived in spring time. It echoed across the room, a mockery of itself in the way it sounded so chilling. She had lifted her head, her odd eyes fixing on Phe.

"You aren't supposed to be in here," she said.

Phe opened her eyes and looked at Karen. She was back in the bedroom. Karen's hair was pushed back, and she was staring into those eyes she'd just been thinking about. They were such a bright blue and the left pupil was permanently blown wide, making it look darker than the other.

Karen had said that it was caused by an accident when she was a girl.

Karen said that it was the reason she could see the dead.

"Hm?"

"You aren't supposed to be in here," Karen repeated, as if reading her very thoughts and knowing exactly where her mind had gone. Phe couldn't help but wonder if they were so connected Karen could do just that. Giving another little sniff, she lifted Phe's hand to cover her chest. Phe could feel Karen's heartbeat, could feel it pumping away beneath her ribcage, so alive.

"I'm sorry," Phe answered. She meant it. Sort of. She wasn't sorry they had met, wasn't sorry that Karen loved her, but she was sorry that this had to hurt so much. She was sorry that they hadn't met before she'd died, when they could have had all the time in the world together.

Karen leaned forward and pressed a kiss to her lips. It was a feeling she'd never get tired of. Karen's mouth was so soft, so sweet and welcoming. If there were an afterlife, a heaven, it'd be this moment stretching on forever.

"Tonight," Karen promised.

"Tonight," Phe agreed, audibly relieved. It was enough to coax a smile to Karen's lips, one that didn't reach her eyes.

"Is it so bad here?" Karen's tone fell short of being teasing.

Phe didn't reply. Couldn't reply. Karen had been the only home, the only family, she had ever cared to know. This apartment had been their escape, their safe haven, their paradise. She was still trapped, though. As soothing as Karen's touch may have been, Phe was still chained to a dead body that no longer felt as if it belonged to her.

Instead of answering, she kissed Karen again, long and slow, and they made love as if it were the last time, because it would be. They spent the day in bed, because Phe knew Karen needed it and because she had nowhere else in the world she would rather be. These were her last hours, her funeral rites found in Karen's skin and the taste of Karen's lips.

It was saying goodbye.

And when the sun had disappeared beyond the city's horizon and the room had fallen dark, the blade was pressed to Phe's throat once more. Karen wasn't crying. She was as calm as she had been in the hospital when she'd been handling that body on the slab. Phe felt the point slide in, bite into flesh and dig deep. She felt blood begin to pour from the wound, hot and wet against her skin as it seeped into the sheets beneath her shoulder. She felt the knife cut to the right with a clean precision.

She felt pain.

She felt how Karen loved her.

She tasted dirt on her tongue.

IN MY DAY...

Wondra Vanian

The 151 out of Brynmawr was safe enough for an elderly woman like Mabel to ride alone at night. Usually.

She clambered up the steps on legs weary from a day's manning a craft stall in the busy Welsh market town and waved her bus pass at an indifferent driver. It was a long old day for someone in her early seventies, but Mabel had promised her best friend of nigh-on-five decades that she would look after the stall until Gladwys was released from the hospital.

She had to make her way right to the back of the bus to find an empty seat, and Mabel's knees screamed in protest as she eased herself into it. The heavy canvas bag she carried dropped onto the seat next to her, nearly spilling its contents. *In my day*, she thought, *we would have given up our seats to an old lady. But I guess times change...*

Taking a deep breath of air that smelled faintly of grease and body odour, Mabel willed herself to relax. It was getting herself worked up over nothing that had landed Gladwys in the hospital with a mild heart attack.

Well, that and the artery-clogging deep-fried food she'd developed a taste for in later years.

The bus *woosh-whumped* into motion. Mabel had to scramble to catch her bag before it fell onto the floor. As they creaked and jerked their way toward the city, Mabel pulled a square of blue knitted fabric from the bag. She unwrapped it, revealing the thin, pointed needles attached. Taking the needles in her expert hands, Mabel added the *click-clack* of knitting to the din of chatter, traffic and muffled music that filled the bus.

It wasn't so bad, filling in at the craft stall – especially since Gladwys always paid in wool. They'd come to the arrangement when they were still blushing newlyweds, giggling over afternoon tea.

'If you babysit for me this weekend,' Gladwys had said, all those years ago, 'I'll shower you in wool.'

'Deal!' Mabel had added, laughing. 'And if you let me borrow that red dress of yours for our date tomorrow night, I'll bake you the best Victoria sponge you've ever tasted.'

Just like that, the currency of their relationship had been set.

Funny thing, time, Mabel mused as she weaved the wool into tidy cables. Those days felt like a million years ago. And yet like they had happened just last week.

A disturbance at the front of the vehicle caught Mabel's attention. They were across from the local college and the engine idled while two girls, fresh-faced and laden with sagging backpacks, tried to exit the bus. Their paths were blocked by a group of raucous young men who forced them backward with menacing sneers.

'Where ya goin', ladies?' the one nearest the girls, beefy and balding, asked. 'Party's just startin'. Ain't it, Richie?'

'That's right, Dai,' a lanky lad called out from the front. 'Gonna have us a good time.'

The one called Richie leaned over the half-door that separated the driver from his passengers. He nabbed the mobile phone resting on the dash and tossed it over his shoulder. Another man caught it and threw it out the open door. It landed on the pavement, bounced and came to rest in several broken pieces.

A woman travelling with her two children stood up, putting herself in front of the teenage girls. 'That's enough,' she said loudly. 'If you don't leave right now, I'm going to phone the—'

Without warning, the man called Dai punched her in the face. She was thrown backward, into the girls she had been trying to protect. All three crumpled to the floor in a tangle of arms and legs.

Chaos ensued. The children screamed. A middle-aged man lunged at the nearest lout, only to have his face brutally smashed against a dirty window. Several people near the front tried to force their way off the bus and were shoved roughly back. Calm only returned when one of the men, bearded and heavily-tattooed, produced a wicked-looking blade and waved it threateningly.

Silence descended in a rush, but for the sound of frightened sobs.

'That's better,' Dai said. 'Now, how's about we take a little ride, eh, drive'?'

Richie grabbed the driver's tie and tugged. 'Hear that, mate? Drive,' he said.

The bus doors closed in a huff of bottled air as the bus pulled away from the curb.

From her place at the back of the bus, Mabel watched the proceedings with a frown. She knew better than to get involved in the altercation; she had enough trouble getting around as it was. While the men made their way up the aisle, demanding the passengers' mobile phones and wallets, Mabel slowly pulled her needles free of the knitting, tucking them under her leg.

'Your turn, granny.'

A man with nervous eyes, younger than both her sons, held out a hand. Mabel obediently reached for her bag. She dug around inside, searching for her phone – not quickly enough, apparently, because he snatched the bag from her, upending it. Her belongings flew everywhere. A ball of double knit rolled down the aisle.

'There was no need for that,' Mabel said disapprovingly. 'I was just about to hand them over.'

His only reply was a scornful laugh. He shook his head as he bent to retrieve her phone and purse, scattering her things even more. As he walked away, the nervous young man stepped on the multi-coloured macaroni chain necklace Mabel's granddaughter had given her the day before. It crunched under his boot.

Mabel gritted her teeth but held her tongue. She made no move to collect her things, more out of fear that she wouldn't be able to get back up than fear of the men who had taken over the bus.

One of the men shouted at the children for crying, which made them cry even louder. Two others fought amongst themselves, shoving each other around in the small space. Richie amused himself by holding his hands in front of the driver's eyes, then pretending to grab the wheel when the driver made to push him away. His beefy friend, Dai, had a pretty, young woman cornered, with his arm across her shoulders and his mouth far too close to her face.

Things had spiralled out of control so quickly. If someone didn't do something soon, a bad situation would likely turn into a tragedy.

Mabel slid her hand toward the needles but stopped when her fingers landed on the half-knitted cardigan she'd been working on. She gathered the material in her fist, smiling.

The ball of wool attached to the knitting was under a seat several rows up, but that didn't matter. Mabel snapped the strand that connected them and pulled a length free. Her knees might be failing her, but her fingers were as agile as ever.

'By the knot of one,' Mabel whispered, finishing the sentence in her mind, *the spell's begun.* She twisted the wool into a knot.

The bus stopped at a red light, giving the driver time to lash out. Richie caught a right fist on the chin and crumpled. He banged his head on a nearby pole as he went down.

'By the knot of two,' *the thought comes true.* Mable tied a second knot below the first.

Dai, the apparent leader of the group, shouted at one of his companions to watch the driver. One of the quarrelling men stumbled – just as the bearded one turned to make his way toward the front of the bus. The bearded man fell onto his friend's knife. His eyes grew wide when he realised the weapon was embedded in his belly.

'By the knot of three,' *justice answer me.*

Chaos erupted. People scrambled to get away from the louts, while *they* scrambled to figure out just what the hell had gone wrong with their busjacking.

'By the knot of four,' *innocents will fear no more.*

Eyes bright with maternal fury, the mother rose. She swung a thick carrier bag at the nearest man, the nervous one who had dumped Mabel's bag. Being rather shorter than his companions, the blow landed on the back of his head. The movement knocked him sideways into the laps of passengers across the aisle, who took advantage of his surprise by pummelling him with their fists.

'By the knot of five,' *trespassers deprive.*

The man nearest the front stepped over Richie's prone form to grab the driver's arm. The bus swerved wildly. Horns blared.

'By the knot of six,' *let wrongs be fixed.*

Dai slapped one of the men who had been quarrelling and ordered him to get his shit together. The other man was on his knees, trying to stem the bright flow of blood seeping from his friend's abdomen.

Not taking kindly to Dai's abuse, the first man lashed out. He struck Dai with a punch that infuriated more than wounded. Dai returned the blow and his companion was knocked back – onto the pair on the floor. Trainers slipping in blood, he scrambled to find his footing.

'By the knot of seven,' *danger lessen.*

He never got the chance. Several passengers descended on him, kicking and stomping until he stopped struggling. Torn between keeping pressure on his friend's wound and stopping another from being assaulted, the kneeling man hesitated a moment too long. A heavy-set woman grabbed him around the neck and dragged him against her seat.

'By the knot of eight,' *worry abate.*

Only two of the busjackers remained a threat: Dai, who screamed at the bus driver to pull over, and a man at the front of the bus, who, struggling against the driver, forced the wheel over. The bus hit the kerb, then ground to a halt.

'By the knot of—'

'Shut up! Everyone shut the fuck up!' Dai shouted. 'Now!'

An echoing *bang* achieved what Dai's words failed to. The passengers froze.

A gun.

It wasn't like they were in America; most of the people on the bus had never even seen a gun in real life – let alone been near one being fired. Ears rang. Hearts pounded wildly in chests. Breaths were held.

'Anyone moves,' Dai said, his eyes looking wildly around the bus, 'they die. Got it?'

Mabel's hands froze on the wool, below the eighth knot.

'Oi, Smithy. Smithy, ya alright?'

Smithy, the bearded man with a knife in his gut, made an odd gurgling noise.

'Shit,' the one at the front said. 'Dai, man, this is bad.'

'Shut up,' Dai replied. 'I'm trying to think.'

'He's *dying*, man.'

'I said shut up!'

'We gotta—'

'I said SHUT THE FUCK UP!' Dai turned the gun on his friend.

With his back to her, Dai was unable to see Mabel deftly tie the wool into a ninth and final knot. Even if he had seen, of course, he wouldn't have known it was his doom. So few people believed in magic these days.

'By the knot of nine,' *let vengeance be mine.*

The thin aluminium needles slid noiselessly from their hiding places. Fast as an arrow, they shot forward, embedding themselves deep in Dai's neck. Shock made his finger tighten on the trigger of the gun. It went off. The other man fell, an 'O' of surprise on his face to match the crimson one blossoming on his forehead.

It took a full heartbeat for the passengers to realise the danger was over. The bus seemed to heave a collective sigh of relief. All eyes turned to the back of the bus, where Mabel folded the half-knitted cardigan into a neat square.

The middle-aged man was on his feet, a frown line etched into his forehead. 'You,' he said in an awed, confused voice. 'How did you...?'

'In my day,' Mabel answered, 'we knew better than to cross a witch.' She sighed. 'But I guess times change. Now,' she added, 'would one of you darlings mind helping me gather my things? My knees aren't what they used to be.'

Several people hurried to oblige.

THE NIGHT OF THE PATRIARCH

Simon Lee-Price

My mother allowed me to play with Billy from around the corner, but she told me never to go into his house. I suspected it was because of his father. Mr Turnbull worked nightshifts and slept the whole day long and whenever Billy and I played football in the street we were always scared we might wake him up. Now and then, I glimpsed him going to work in the dark. Always he wore the same clompy boots and flat cap and kept his hands shoved inside the pockets of his donkey jacket. Only once did I catch sight of him in the daylight. It was a Sunday morning and he was trudging toward me with a heavy sack over his shoulder. His face was lumpy and unshaven. I moved out into the road and he turned and glared at me as he went past. That look frightened me, made me feel I'd done something wrong, and I told my mother about it. She comforted me and explained I wasn't to blame for anything. Men like Mr Turnbull always mistrusted newcomers.

Not long afterwards my mother shocked me by saying I would have to stay at Billy's house for the evening. She had an important appointment and the girl who usually sat up with me was ill. She must have seen the expression of terror on my face because she stroked my hair and tried to reassure me. Mr Turnbull would already have left for work by the time she dropped me off, she said, and she would be back to collect me long before he returned from his nightshift. She told me I could trust Mrs Turnbull who, although she was very strict, was a fair and decent woman. All day I was afraid. I even thought about running away. But my mother knew how to persuade me and promised to bring back a present for me if I agreed to stay with the Turnbulls.

Billy's house was in a sloping row of red-brick terraces. It was older and smaller than our house and when I went inside I discovered they didn't even have a proper kitchen, just a space for cooking at the back of the living room behind a partition. The TV was away getting repaired, so Billy and I played with Matchbox cars on the rug in front of the gas fire and drank the raspberry pop my mother had given me. Then we read war comics. Billy was bad at reading. Even when he spoke he mixed up his words. He soon got bored and rolled on his back.

'Are you an only child?' he asked me, even though he already knew.

I said nothing and just kept my face in the comic.

'Why doesn't your mam have more children?'

I felt myself getting angry with him. 'Because,' I said.

'Don't you wish you had a big brother like our Gareth?'

'No thanks. He always gives you dead legs.'

'Why doesn't your dad live with you?'

Mrs Turnbull stepped out from behind the partition. Her flabby forearms were wet and red, and she waved a scrubbing brush at both of us, even though Billy had started it all.

'You two boys, cut out that loose talk.'

We lay reading our comics again, in silence, until eventually I needed to go to the toilet. I stood up and asked where it was. Billy told me to go upstairs and as I left the room he called over in an American voice, 'Just yell if you need anything.'

The stairs were steep and narrow, and the tatty old carpet did not reach the edges. The toilet was the first door at the top, and further along the landing were two other doors, both closed. As well as Gareth, who was in the Army, Billy had two bossy older sisters and I wondered where they all slept at night. At home I had a whole bedroom to myself and we had a spare room as well.

After I'd been to the toilet, my curiosity got the better of me. I just wanted to see how many people could fit inside a bedroom. I stood before the nearest door and raised my hand to knock, just in case one of his sisters had secretly come home. But I couldn't think of what I'd say if I got an answer. Anyway, I was sure if somebody had come into the house I'd have heard them from the living room. I turned the handle and slowly pushed the door open. Even with the light from the landing the room was almost black, so I reached inside and felt along the wall for the light switch. The bulb must have been old because it fizzed and flickered as it came on and it was very dim. In the corner facing me was a tall brown wardrobe and next to it a chest of drawers with Billy's plastic soldiers on top, lined up and pointing their guns at me. Iron bunkbeds stood against both walls with just enough floor space between then for a fluffy rug. There was no carpet, only bare floorboards. I noticed a bright white nightie spread out on a bottom bunk, and a soppy *Grease* poster hung on the wall. At the end of the room, in front of the curtains, was a dressing table and mirror, all cluttered with brushes and sprays and make-up, just like my mother's messy dressing table at home. I switched off the light again and quietly pulled the door to. I had seen enough. Now I could tease Billy and say he had to share a room with girls.

But I was curious about the other room. It had to be where Mr and Mrs Turnbull slept. I approached the door, very nervous. I would be in trouble if they caught me nosing around in there. I glanced over my shoulder, fearing Billy or his mum had crept to the top of the stairs and was watching me. Sure I was alone, I reached toward the handle, a wooden knob, not a lever like the other one. Just as my fingers were about to grip, the knob began to turn. The door opened slowly inward. My hand frozen in front of me, I stared at the dark gap growing wider and wider. Then an electric bolt shot through my body. I turned and sped along the landing and all the way down the stairs.

Billy glanced up at me from the rug as I came into the living room. My heart was still pounding and I tried to control my breathing. I had the feeling the two of them had been talking about me. They must have grown suspicious about why I'd taken so much time just to use the toilet. I sat down and picked up a car and rolled it back and forth along the edge of the hearth. I kept thinking about what had appeared in the doorway as I ran down the stairs. It was a man like Mr Turnbull but half-naked and with something wet and glistening on his body. I felt afraid to ask Billy who it was up in the room because his mum was hovering nearby. I was sure it was some kind of family secret I wasn't supposed to know about.

I kept my eye on the clock on the mantelpiece and promised myself I would never set foot in this house again. At around nine Billy's mum made us some cocoa. I looked at her face as she held the mug down to me. Did she have to go into that front bedroom to sleep, I wondered. She had greasy grey hair and she suddenly appeared very old and fierce. Crow's feet spread from the corners of her eyes and her front teeth were yellow or missing. She could have been a witch and I was glad my mother was young and beautiful.

The cocoa tasted different from what I was used to, but it was sweet, and I drank it down to the sludge. Afterwards Billy and I played Top Trumps and his mother sat on the couch sewing patches on a raggedy pair of trousers. I listened out for any sounds on the stairs. I started to think the man I'd seen might have been a trick of the light. If it was Mr Turnbull and he was awake, why did he hide upstairs?

More than an hour was left before my mother was due to pick me up. I hated her for leaving me with the Turnbulls, but I would forgive her if she brought me an exciting present. I tried guessing what it might be – a cap gun, a cowboy hat and holster. Then I couldn't believe it. Out of the blue I needed to go to the toilet again. I squeezed my legs together and hinted to Billy to see if he needed to use the toilet too so I wouldn't have to go upstairs alone this time. He played dumb and a mean grin spread across his face. I noticed he'd hardly touched his cocoa.

I went out into the hall and switched on the light, which I couldn't even remember turning off. Step by step, I climbed the stairs, stopping each time they made a creak. The bedroom door was closed now. I kept my eyes on it all the way to the bathroom and locked myself inside. There was a small window and I opened it, thinking it would be good for making an escape. I leant over the sink and put my head out. It was very high up and I could see no drainpipe to shimmy down.

After I'd finished and pulled the chain, I heard something on the other side of the door. It sounded like a person walking. Then the noise stopped, as if they knew I was listening to them. I held my breath, sure they were standing right outside. Billy's words came back to me. *Just yell if you need anything.* He must have known about the front bedroom. That somebody was in there who might come out. I sucked in air and got ready to shout. A voice came from beyond the door.

'What are you doing? Come out of there.'

It sounded like Mrs Turnbull. I hoped so and that it wasn't somebody copying her voice.

'I know you're in there, Daniel.'

As I went to slide back the bolt, I heard a man's voice, further away but very loud and gruff. 'Bring that boy to me.'

The handle rattled. 'Open this door.'

'I want to go home.' The words came out as a squeak. My heart was beating in my throat. I stood with my back against the door, facing the open window and the dark night outside.

The man began to bawl. I couldn't understand every word but he was saying terrible things about me and my mother and that she would soon be here so they needed to hurry.

The handle rattled again. 'If you don't open this door Mr Turnbull will break it down.'

The bolt was flimsy. I had seen on cop shows how grown men charged doors with their shoulder and made them burst open. I stepped over to the window, but I already knew I didn't have the guts to climb. I slid back the bolt and opened the door.

Mrs Turnbull was waiting halfway along the landing. She beckoned to me with her finger, the same way she would call Billy in from the street. Beyond her the bedroom door stood wide open. I thought I could make a run for it, down the stairs to the front door. But Billy had come up and was blocking my way. He held a hard plastic dagger and pointed the tip at me.

'Go on,' he said. 'It's only Pa.'

I thought if I did what they ordered it might go better for me. I had nowhere to run. My only hope was that my mother would get here soon. I approached Mrs Turnbull and she moved aside to let me pass. I could already see into the room. There was a double bed with somebody big sitting on the edge, but it was too dark in there to tell if it was Mr Turnbull. A bad smell came out, sweaty and similar to dogs when they get wet. I held my hand over my nose and mouth. As I reached the doorway, a lamp came on, very dim, but enough for me to see it was not really a bedroom and more like inside an allotment shed. Strange cutting tools hung from the wall and cans and boxes lined rows of shelves going up to the ceiling. Stacked on the floor were some fat grey sacks and under a workbench I saw a tin bath with dirty towels draped over the side.

Mr Turnbull sat on the edge of the bed wearing only white long johns. His belly was blown up like a beach ball and something silver was growing all over his bare skin. Around his feet lay a mess of what I first thought were giant potato peelings. In his hand he was holding a metal tool and now he placed the blade against the side of his shoulder and pressed it in. His expression didn't change as he sliced away a curl of silver down to his elbow. He took it between two fingers and tossed it to the floor.

'You love your mother?' he asked, looking at me for the first time, his beard grown thick, his eyes black and shiny.

I nodded furiously.

He cut into his arm again and peeled away more of the scaly growth. A fly had started to buzz around him. He laughed. 'They find me, even at this time of year.'

The sight of him made the sick rise to the back of my throat. 'Let me go home,' I managed to say.

'You can't.' He stood up, still holding the tool. 'You can never go home again.'

At that moment the doorbell rang.

'That's her,' said Mrs Turnbull in a hissing voice from the landing.

Mr Turnbull put a finger to his lips. His gaze switched from me to the workbench and the bath underneath. It was my last chance. I took one step backward, then I turned and ran.

'Grab him,' he shouted. 'Don't let him get to her.'

I dodged past Mrs Turnbull's hands. But Billy caught me by the back of my sweater and dragged me to the floor. He pressed himself on top of me, breathing his eggy breath right up my nose. Usually I could beat him at wrestling, but he seemed to have got super-human strength from somewhere or I had grown weak. He smothered my mouth with his palm as I tried to cry out and his mum helped him to hold me down, her fingers pinching through my clothes into the skin.

'Freeze,' said Billy, 'or I'll pump you full of lead.'

The bell rang four or five times. Then silence. I thought of my mother and if I would ever see her again. I prayed she knew I was in danger and had gone to call the police. Together Billy and his mum lifted me to my feet and hauled me back into the bedroom.

Mr Turnbull was standing at the window. He held back a curtain and was looking down into the street.

'Have you ever seen a demon?' he said, without turning around.

I screamed and tried to fight free. But Billy and his mother held me firmly by my arms and legs.

'Not me,' he said. 'I'm no demon, despite what you may think.' He signalled to his wife. 'Bring him here.'

They led me around the bed and stood me next to him. Up close the silver stuff looked like the shiny backs of thousands of tiny beetles huddled together. He grabbed me by the hair and pointed my face at the window.

'That way,' he said, 'there, at the top of the street.'

As my eyes adjusted to the dark, I saw my mother near the street corner. I recognised her fur coat and long hair. She was walking away very slowly, and I could tell she was sad and probably crying. I felt a pain go through my heart for not trying harder and letting Billy get the better of me. Now I was a prisoner of the Turnbull family and she would be childless. I banged my fist on the window, but it hardly made a sound. Mr Turnbull grabbed my arms and pinned them against my body.

'Watch,' he said, 'just watch.'

Through my tears, I could see my mother had stopped under a street lamp, which lit her up a pale orange. She dug her hands in her hair and then started pulling it.

'He's frightened enough already,' shouted Mrs Turnbull. 'Just get him out of my house. Billy, run downstairs and open the back door.'

'He needs to know,' said Mr Turnbull. 'He has to see it for himself.'

While they spoke, I watched my poor mother tugging at her hair and stamping her feet on the pavement. Then from behind the end house, something dark and spindly appeared. It was almost as high as the roof and walked stiffly on two legs like a man on stilts. I didn't know how it could keep its balance because the upper half slanted forward, the way I'd seen old men with their walking sticks. It had jagged wings instead of arms and a massive pink head. A horn grew out at the back of the head and its long, curved chin made its ugly face seem to smile. My mother carried on pulling her hair and stomping. She had no idea it was behind her, even when it was practically hanging over her.

I rubbed the water out of my eyes. I could have been watching a pantomime. I felt giddy, ready to burst out laughing. 'What is that big thing behind her?'

'*That* is a demon,' said Mr Turnbull.

It bent lower and its mouth dropped open like a dog about to eat. 'Run!' I shouted to my mother. 'Run!'

Instead of running, my mother turned around and looked up at the monster. Its eyes grew bigger and turned fiery yellow.

'She serves him and calls him Patriarch.'

I watched my mother talk to it. Its big head hung still, as if it were listening to her, but at the back of its body a tail curled up and started swinging.

'They are talking about you, Daniel. She has promised you to him tonight.'

'The backdoor's open,' said Billy, panting. 'Run for your life, Danny Boy.'

'Get out of here,' said his mum. 'I don't want her bringing any demon to this house.'

'You're all liars.' I shook my head. 'I don't believe you.'

'Then believe your eyes.' Mr Turnbull crouched down, the bones in his knees cracking. 'Look at my body. This is what happens when a demon touches you.'

I shut my eyes and held my breath. It was too disgusting. Too unbelievable.

'I was eight like you when he touched me.'

Mrs Turnbull joined in. 'There's no cure. He has to cut that stuff away every day and lie in a bath of chemicals.'

'Soon it will cover me from head to toe.'

I opened my eyes. In the places where he'd peeled away the silver, his skin was already turning lumpy. The silver had reached his face too. I could see it even through his beard and beneath the cream he wore. I looked out of the window again. The creature and my mother were gone. I pressed my cheek against the glass so I could see if they'd crossed to this side of the street.

'Why has she promised me to a demon?'

'So she can stay young and beautiful.'

'How do you know?'

He stood up. 'She's my mother too.'

I still refused to believe him. Even so, I wanted to draw the curtains closed and hide in another room. If the doorbell had rung and my mother had called my name, I'd never have gone down the stairs. The sound I heard was far more terrifying. Even Mr Turnbull sprang back from the window. It was a scream. So loud and shrill the glass shook. It came from all directions at once, not one scream but more like hundreds of shrieking voices fighting against one another. When it finally stopped the silence felt slow and unreal. I swallowed and looked across at Billy, who still had his hands pressed over his ears.

Outside, lights went on in the other houses and people began to come out into the street.

'What now, John?' said Mrs Turnbull. 'What does that mean?'

Mr Turnbull said nothing. His dark eyes looked half-scared, half-sad. He put on his work clothes and heavy boots and went down the stairs. We followed him.

'Stay close to me,' he said, opening the front door.

The street was full of people. Women wearing nightgowns and slippers, children in their pyjamas and coats. Some of the men carried cricket bats and iron bars. Everybody was heading in one direction, toward the corner where I'd seen my mother and the creature. A big crowd had gathered in the road in front of my house. People must have heard the scream for miles around and poured here from the surrounding streets. The crowd was calmer than at a football match and people talked in low voices.

Mrs Turnbull stayed behind at the edge of the crowd with one of her daughters who'd found us, but Mr Turnbull took me and Billy by the hand and led us deeper into the press of bodies.

'How did you escape from the demon?' I asked him.

'There were two of us. I had a twin sister.'

Billy poked his head around his dad's belly to look at me. 'Holy cow! I've just worked it out. You're my uncle.'

We found our way through to the space in the centre of the crowd, right outside my house. It was the very spot where Billy and I played with our Action Men. An old woman lay curled up on her side on the pavement. She was wearing my mother's fur coat and best red dress. Somebody aimed a bright torch at her face. The skin was shrivelled to the bone and the eyes were gone. Her hair was just a few tufts of white cotton wool. She looked like she had been dead for hundreds of years.

LENA'S GHOST

Nico Bell

Lena's thumb traced the ridges of her detective badge. It hung from her neck, a heavy pledge to do the right thing; and as youngest detective in her precinct, it served as a constant reminder that everyone was watching her. An odor of sweat mixed with mold seeped from the prison walls while a sense of hopelessness soured the air. She'd sent plenty of women to this filthy place, but today she wore a visitor's badge, sat in the hard chair across the table, kept her eyes focused on her lap and waited.

The clank of the woman's handcuffs on the metal tabletop served as an introduction. "This is a nice surprise," she said. Two decades behind bars hadn't tarnished Lena's mother's dry southern twang. "Did someone die?"

"What? No. Why would you think that, Barbara?" – Lena wasn't in the habit of addressing her mother as Mom.

Her mother shrugged. "How many times have you come to visit? Four? Maybe five? And when you have graced me with your royal presence, it's always bad news."

Lena steadied her rapid pulse with a deep breath. "I need your help."

"Seriously?" Barbara let out a single huff. "Did you hear that Ms. Correction Officer? My baby girl needs my help."

"Settle down, inmate." The burly woman standing guard at the door crossed her arms over her chest.

"She's happy for me." Barbara turned her focus back to Lena. "The guards don't show emotion, but this one here, she likes me. Ain't that right, Ms. Correction Officer?"

The woman's jaw tightened and looked to Lena. "You need me, I'll be on the other side of the door." She left as Barbara chuckled.

"This is serious." Lena leaned forward. "I know we've never talked about that night, but I need to know the truth."

For a second, something flickered across her mother's aged face. A flash of concern, maybe even regret. But it vanished into the folds of her wrinkled forehead. "Now, why would I want to go dredging up that old memory?"

Lena looked into Barbara's pale blue eyes. "You killed three men in one night. I need to know why."

"Oh come on, Buttercup. You're a fancy detective, after all. You can look up everything there is to know about my case."

"Humor me." Lena tried to steady her voice, but a tremble punctuated her words. She prayed her mother hadn't noticed. "Just for once, be a mom and help your daughter. Or if that's too much work, how about trying to be a decent human being and tell the truth?"

Barbara's eyes widened and then narrowed into small slits until her brows pierced together. "You got some nerve. You think you're better than me, don't you?" she said.

"I *am* better than you."

"You're clueless. That's the truth. And when it comes to justice, honey, you're only scratching the surface with that shiny badge."

"Then tell me." Lena balanced on the edge of her seat. "The men you killed, did you know them beforehand?"

"Really? Listen up, Buttercup—,"

"Don't call me that." She clipped the words.

"Sorry," Barbara sighed. "No, I didn't know them, but you knew that already."

"And you got drunk?"

"You know I did. Look, why don't you just spit out what this is all about? Why the sudden desire to drive down memory lane? What's going on, Lena?"

Lena ran her hand down her face, tucked her long black hair behind her ear and focused on her mother's eyes. "The incident report states you had alcohol and hallucinogenic drugs in your system at the time of your arrest."

"Apparently."

"And you stated that you saw two teenagers standing behind the men."

Her mother turned her face away, focusing her gaze on the side wall. "Following them," she mumbled.

Lena's stomach churned. "Right. Okay, you said they followed the men into the party. Stood beside them the whole time."

"Something like that."

"And at some point, you went into the kitchen, grabbed a butcher's knife from the block and stabbed one of the men."

"If that's what the report says."

"Barbara." The anger boiled over. Lena slammed her open palm on the table. "This is important."

Barbara stared at Lena's hand, fingers sprawled out on the tabletop. "Yeah, I stabbed him. After that, I'm not sure what happened. Chaos, really. And at some point, I blacked out."

"Okay." Lena took her hand from the table and squeezed it in the other to try and stop them both from shaking.

"I'd do it again, you know."

"Yeah, so you've said once or twice. What about the teenagers? There's not much else said about them other than they were part of the group."

Barbara chewed her lower lip.

"Who were they? Why did you feel it was important to mention your hallucinations?"

"Hallucinations." The word stretched from her mother's throat. "Every day I think of those boys."

"Barbara." Lena's mind scrambled for the right words, but any attempt to form her question – the one she'd driven hours to get an answer for – only got jumbled in the back of her throat. "Do you remember those boys or do you... Were they... Can you remember if...?"

"What?"

"Nothing." Lena waved away the question. "Forget it. McKenna was right."

"McKenna?"

Lena cursed.

"Ah." Barbara gave a slow nod. "Yet another part of your life you don't want your mother to know about. I get it."

"I won't waste any more of your precious time." She pushed back the chair and stood. A parade of unspoken swear words marched through her head. How could she have thought this was a good idea? Her mother was sick, a murderer. What sort of help could Barbara ever give?

"Wait. Please." Her mother slid to the edge of her chair. "You see them, don't you? You want to know if what I saw was really a hallucination or if it's possible for a person to see ghosts. Am I right?"

Pressure mounted behind Lena's eyes, and she bit her lip to keep it from trembling. "I'm not sure what I see. For all I know, you could have some mental illness that got passed to me. Or maybe that night, it really was just the booze and drugs whipping up imaginary people in your mind. And maybe what I see is just a result of sleep deprivation."

"Well, I can help you with some of that. You're not crazy. At least, not because of some genetic stuff. I've seen plenty of psychologists over the last few decades and not one of them says I'm batty." She motioned her head toward the empty seat. "Go on. Sit back down, honey. I'll tell you anything you want to know, hand to God. But first, I want you to answer one question."

Lena's chest tightened, but she sat. "What?"

"How many people are in this room?"

"Well, um…" Lena looked into the creamy eyes of the others, the eyes she'd been trying to avoid since her mother entered the room. "There's you and me."

"Okay, Einstein. Anyone can see us. Who else?"

Lena frowned. "The men from the party. All three of them."

Her mother nodded. "And?"

"And two women. One with a gash on her head, another with blood-soaked clothes. Both in prison jumpsuits."

Her mother let out a long slow breath like a balloon releasing air from a pin-pricked hole. "How long have you been able to see these types of folks?"

"You mean ghosts?" Lena laughed without humor as a rouge tear ran down her cheek. She wiped it with the back of her hand. "Not long."

"I'm sorry, Buttercup. I really am. I don't know how I got this way, but I always hoped you'd never be like me."

And the way Barbara's shoulders slumped forward, the way her lips curved down, made Lena think that maybe, just this once, her mother spoke the truth.

"But now you've got a responsibility. Same as myself."

"What are you talking about?" Lena shook her head. "Are you saying I should start killing people the way you did? No way. Never."

Barbara's lips pursed together.

"Never." Lena spat the word in her mother's face.

"Have the ghosts shown you their deaths?"

Lena's mouth dropped open.

"Yeah, I didn't think so. Let them touch you. They'll show you how they died." Barbara lowered her head. Her voice soft. "No. That doesn't describe it right. They'll let you experience it." Moisture clouded her eyes as she focused on Lena. "Then you can judge me."

"That's what happened at the party."

It wasn't really a question, but Barbara nodded. "I thought I'd lost my mind when I first saw them, but they put their hands on my arm and then everything made sense." She rested her elbows on the table. "Their murders would never have been solved."

"You don't know that."

"Really? Have you looked into it?"

Lena slumped. She'd read the report. The men her mother killed were suspects in an alleged robbery gone fatally wrong. The teens where in the wrong place at the wrong time. But there wasn't enough evidence to make the murder charges stick.

"Oh Buttercup," Barbara sighed. "I'd never felt rage like that. Those teenagers, they demanded action, and I wasn't capable of controlling myself. After that night, it took time to adjust, just like it will take time for you as well, but you'll be able to channel the anger and pick your battles."

"No." Lena looked at her badge. "There's always another way. New evidence to find, DNA, a witness, something."

"If that were true, you wouldn't be here asking my permission. Tell me. Whose ghost do you see?"

Her pulse quickened.

"Ah, okay." Barbara nodded. "It's someone you know. A coworker? A friend?"

"I see a lot of ghosts. Apparently, it's a new perk of the job."

"Then arrest the people responsible, if it's that easy, then work within the law and make it happen."

Lena pinched the bridge of her nose. "I think... I can't be sure, but from what I've experienced, the ghosts are of those who will never get justice through the system."

"Then is what you need to do so bad? Is what I did so bad?"

"Stop." Lena steadied her nerves and made a conscious effort to replace the wobble in her tone with the confidence she'd long ago planted in herself and harvested for years. "I'm different than you."

"Honey, under the right circumstances, anyone can be like me."

Lena's throat tightened because hadn't she seen that exact thing over and over since becoming a cop?

The guard opened the door, poking her head over the threshold. "Wrap it up, ladies."

Lena leaned forward. "Was it worth it? Was losing your freedom, your entire life, worth killing those men? Think of all the lives you've destroyed."

Barbara's smile spread to her eyes. "You seem to be doing just fine."

"But your dreams? All flushed away. What good are you to anyone behind bars?"

The guard stepped in and took Barbara by the arm. Lena jumped to her feet, a desperation clawed under her skin as she fought the urge to grab her mother's shoulders and shake her.

"Please, Mom. I don't know what to do." Lena's words hung in the air between them.

Barbara looked over her shoulder, a softness in her eyes. "It's okay, Buttercup. Just do the right thing."

* * *

The wind slapped Lena's cheeks as she stepped out of the prison. McKenna leaned against her car, her pink lipstick kissing the rim of her cigarette.

"I thought you quit." Lena took it out of her girlfriend's hand, took a puff and handed it back.

"How did it go?" McKenna flicked the rest of the cigarette to the ground, grinding it with her boot.

"I don't know. It was weird, I guess." Lena took McKenna's hand, but the familiar warmth offered no comfort.

"Yeah, I can imagine. I still can't understand why you'd want to visit after all this time."

Lena shrugged. "I thought she could help me on a case." The lie slipped out so naturally.

"Well, did she?"

Lena let her eyes fall to the ghost standing next to McKenna. Three-year-old Thomas, McKenna's son. The son McKenna claimed her ex-girlfriend kidnapped. The son Lena spent days and resources investigating and searching for all over the city. And now Thomas stood with those milky eyes and pale skin, head tilted up toward Lena.

He reached out his hand.

McKenna rubbed Lena's arm. "Hey, are you okay? You've been off a little these past few days."

Thomas stepped forward. The thumping of Lena's heart echoed through her ears. For a second he paused, but when Lena made no move to stop him he placed his tiny hand on top of hers. A freezing tidal wave rippled over her skin; her brain sizzled with his memories.

McKenna and her ex were fighting in their apartment's living room.

Thomas cowering in the corner, curled in a tiny ball, hugging his fluffy stuffed kitten.

Lena withered and slumped to the pavement as fear crept through her veins.

Through his veins.

"Babe." McKenna dropped to one knee and gripped Lena's shoulders. "What's wrong?"

Lena watched McKenna's ex point to Thomas, saying something about never wanting to be a parent.

Screaming. Stomping. The front door slams.

The ex leaves.

Gone forever. McKenna cries into her palms.

And Thomas cries because he doesn't know what's going on except that one of his parents just walked out.

"He's so confused," Lena whispered.

"What did you say? Baby, talk to me. What do you need?"

A tightness wrapped around Lena as she saw McKenna begin to squeeze Thomas. So many curse words, so much anger being hurled at his precious little soul.

And then McKenna's hands wrapped around her son's throat. Except when it was over, when McKenna let go, she thought her son had taken his last breath. But he was still alive. He was still alive when she dumped his body in that shallow grave.

"Stop!" Lena's entire body vibrated with panic as she gasped for a single speck of oxygen.

McKenna cupped her hands around Lena's face. "Breathe, babe. Relax. It's going to be okay. You're having a panic attack."

"No." Lena rested her head against the car. Thomas stood in front of her and let go of her hand. "It's not okay."

"You're under a lot of stress. You've been working every waking minute trying to find Thomas, and then seeing your mom... What happened in there? What did your mom do to you?" McKenna's hands smoothed back Lena's hair.

"The truth." Lena's voice was barely above a whisper. "Mom told me the truth."

"I knew this was a bad idea. You need to promise never to come back. That woman is poison. She triggered something, didn't she? She's driving you crazy."

Lena shook her head and rubbed her throat. "I loved you for so long, McKenna."

McKenna wrapped her arms around Lena. "I love you too."

Lena buried her face into her girlfriend's hair, inhaling the sweet scent of strawberry shampoo. When she untangled herself she looked at Thomas.

"I'm going to come back here. Visit my mom more regularly."

"No, Lena. Don't."

"Turns out, she's useful. She helped me."

"Really?" McKenna's eyes widened.

"She answered my question."

"So driving all the way up here, taking time off work, driving yourself crazy just to see her face-to-face… it's all worth it?"

Lena closed her eyes.

Under the right circumstances, anyone can be like me.
Just do the right thing.

Lena allowed her body to harden, a sense of numbness to blanket her. "Yes. It's worth it."

DOMESTIC DISTURBANCE

Horace Torys

Today's the day I murder my husband.

And with that happy realization, I get out of bed. I've got an outfit all picked out in the closet. It's a vintage number, a yellow rain slicker with attached hood, and matching gloves and boots, which I take down from the hanger and carry to the bathroom. Got an alibi, a good story, and a disposal method. Haven't decided the weapon yet, but we've got a kitchen full of knives, a garage full of tools, and shed out back full of yard work implements. It'll come to me when the time is right.

I check my makeup in the bathroom mirror and pull up the yellow hood, sleeves rustling as I fasten it in place. I pull on the gloves, snapping them into place. I hear a thump from the kitchen downstairs and turn, flicking off the light. It's time to go see Hal.

At the top of the stairwell, I hear a bellow of rage, which makes me pause. He usually waits till afternoon to get drunk and worked up that bad. I hear him pound down the hallway, calling me several choice epithets at full volume. I hadn't planned for this.

He charges up the stairs. "You psycho! You think you can scare me by putting some dead hobo dressed like me in the broom closet? I'll show you scared!"

Dead hobo? The absurdity of it all has me frozen on the top step, and then he crashes into me, hands around my throat, slamming me into the wall hard enough that I see stars, pinning me up against the floral wallpaper so my feet can't reach the ground. We've been here before, but I've never seen him as unhinged as this. I think he might mean it this time.

Just before I think I'm going to black out, I manage a swift yellow-booted kick to his groin. He drops me, falling to his knees, breathless. I cough a few times, then place a boot on his stupid balding forehead and heave, toppling him into the stairwell. There's a series of carpet-muffled thumps, followed by a distinct crack as he hits the bottom. My slicker feels suddenly hot, and I peel it off, along with the gloves and boots, coughing a few more times. I settle my hair.

I walk down and stand on the last step. Sure enough, he's lying there in his dirty undershirt and plaid boxers, not breathing, head twisted nearly backwards. I didn't really get to appreciate the moment.

I step over him.

Padding down the hall into the kitchen, I see a coffee cup spilled on the floor and the corner closet is ajar. There's a foot keeping the door from closing. I walk over and open it. Slumped inside in a semi-seated position is a man dressed in a stained undershirt and plaid boxers, missing his head. The bloody neck stump is all congealed, so he must have been there some time. As the door bangs against the wall, the man tips forward, and I see stuffed behind him is Hal's head with his stupid bald spot. I look back toward the stairs. Hal's still there, dead.

My disposal plan will still work here, though. I go to the garage for the tarp and rope. The smell is overpowering, flies buzzing everywhere. Our SUV is crashed into the back wall, chunks of drywall and caked brain on the hood. A hairy leg clad in plaid boxers protrudes from under the front tire. The driver door is open, a deflated airbag spilling from the steering wheel into the empty seat, the keys in the ignition, gauge on empty.

But I'm here for the tarp. I reach under the workbench, and nothing. I look. It's gone. Maybe Hal had it in the back of the SUV for gardening. I pop the hatch. Another, fresher Hal tumbles out, cascading off a pile of bloated gray Hals.

I wander through the open garage door to our long, tree-lined driveway. There's the rope, anyway, twisting in the wind with the weight of three Hals on the nearest bare-limbed walnut. Another Hal's floating in the koi pond. And one naked one's just half-buried in the lawn. Head first.

Holding my breath, I walk back through the garage to the kitchen. I can do it without the tarp. I go to the stairs and hunker down beside him, gripping under his armpits. I pull, and his head lolls as I slide him across the linoleum. It gets too cumbersome that way, so I go around and grab his feet, and angle him around, skirting the kitchen island. Reaching the side door, I open it and prop open the screen door. I wrest him onto the stoop and down the three steps, savoring each bang of his skull on the stairs. The concrete walk is too rough, so I angle him onto the grass to make dragging him along easier, and we slither into the back yard, past a charred corpse near the grill and another draped in the birdbath.

This month, after much nagging and threatening, Hal finally got our in-ground pool drained and covered for the winter, and it will make an apropos final resting place for him. I go to the deep end, cast aside some of the weights and flip back the cover. The stench hits me like a sledgehammer. I collapse on the tile walkway, wracked with dry heaves. My vision blurs with tears.

Wiping them away, I roll over and peer at the pool again.

Huh.

Well, Hal was nothing if not predictable.

This end of the pool is piled to the five-foot marker with rotting middle-aged women, about half in pajamas, half in yellow slickers, with a few in bathrobes or cocktail dresses or pantsuits, and one in a clown costume I bought once for an office Halloween party.

Huh.

I'm distracted by a gurgle behind me, and I turn to see a not-so-dead-after-all Hal bring a pool cover weight down on my skull.

* * *

Today's the day I murder my husband.

And with that happy realization, I get out of bed.

BLACK FLOWERS

Philip Charter

Sidney cut the roses with the secateurs and tossed the stems onto the pile on the floor. You had to cut them back hard to keep them fresh. Hopefully, it would turn things around for the wilting flowers. The sparse drum beat of The Cure echoed through the florist's shop as the town outside slowly came to life. Monday morning.

Fulfilling orders, managing stock and arranging the displays: it was too much for one person. Worst of all, you had to deal with the customers. One stood outside the front door now, peering in. The old bag in the headscarf rapped on the glass door.

'Are you open?' she asked, revealing an extraordinarily gummy mouth.

'No. Not yet.' Sidney hated the 'early birds'.

'Oh, but... I'm ever so sorry—'

The family had moved here from London for the peace and quiet, but it turned out that Truro was a town like any other – guilty men buying bouquets, rich Bristolians getting married and old people dying. And now a toothless crone standing outside the front door at

8.38am, begging to be let in. Some people had a bloody nerve. 'What do you want?'

It was Fran who had suggested opening a shop; flowers always sold, and people in this part of the world still valued the personal touch. Sidney had never been one for frilly things in life, but now Fran was living back in London with Charlie, the only option was to hold things down until they saw sense and got the family back together.

The reluctant florist sighed and unlocked the front door. The bell jingled merrily as the woman scurried inside. She wasted no time in sharing every detail of the 'worst week of her life'. Her Arthur was gone and there had been 'ever so much paperwork'. At least someone else was miserable too.

Why the hell should flower sellers have to smile and provide sparkling conversation? Especially when their family had done a runner after one misunderstanding. It was only a few threats and a dead crow in the mail, for God's sake. Sidney had done it *for them*, to put a hex on the new shop sucking the life out of *their family*'s business. But that was it – divorce pending and custody of Charlie gone. At least Fran had stopped short of citing the Mental Health Act. Sidney was more stable now, getting things together.

'It's a bit dreary in here, isn't it? And I don't like that music,' said the old lady, who turned out to be called Mrs Godbeer. 'Something smells nasty too.'

'I haven't had a chance to bin the cuttings yet, and the music stays.'

'When I came in here last year the displays were colourful: lilies and carnations. And there was none of that *voodoo* stuff over there. It's unchristian.'

'Well, we're an alternative florists now. Haven't you seen the new name? Black Flowers. We've got some lovely dahlias, midnight pansies and black magic hollyhocks.'

Mrs Godbeer didn't look impressed.

'Listen, lady, times change. Black is the new black,' said Sidney, forcing a smile.

'Oh dear. I just need a basic wreath, you see.'

'I'd recommend one of our funeral packages. Take a pamphlet.'

'It's all a bit gothic, dear. My Arthur loved bright colours, roses and the like. I think I better get a second opinion.'

What a waste of time, and after opening early for her as well. One way or another, the shop would convert this town of fussy traditionalists. Monochrome flowers could be beautiful too, thought Sidney. 'Alright, Mrs Godbeer. You come back if you change your mind.' She was probably heading straight down to Occasions, to see that pandering ponce of a flower merchant, Prunella Smyth. She might think the war was over after the court upheld the restraining order, but Sidney was just getting started. Things had been much simpler when there was only the one florist in town.

Gummy Godbeer muttered something on the way out. Her friends in the Rotary Club wouldn't be passing by. Big deal. When gothic became fashionable again Black Flowers would make the magazines, be heralded as a trailblazer.

It was somewhat strange that a practising Satanist had ended up as a florist. Cornwall's pagan tradition had always fascinated Sidney, and things had been good for a while, then Fran voiced doubts about the books, the clothes and the spells. Apparently, some of the kids at school were teasing Charlie.

The people in Truro expected florists to look like Prunella Smyth – horsey women with perfect teeth and antique jewellery. They were unaccustomed to dealing with people with spiky hair and skull rings like Sidney.

After work, Sidney went upstairs to the flat above the shop. Tomorrow was Tuesday, which was a busy day in Truro. With yet another delayed mortgage instalment due, Sidney considered making a few concessions to increase cash flow until the busier summer season started. Would it be best to remove the books, candles and amulets? No. It was important to push the agenda; not all florists should offer namby-pamby bouquets and conform to type.

To make matters worse, there was a leaflet from Smyth's shop smiling up from the doormat. Rage boiled. Was it not possible to fail at having a family and running a business, and not have your face rubbed in it when you came home?

A well-worn copy of Poe's *The Murders in the Rue Morgue* lay open on the coffee table. Sidney knew every gory detail of the locked room murder. It had sparked an interest in death that had stayed with Sidney since reading it as a 16-year-old. A particular passage of text sprang to mind.

> *...the party made its way into a small paved yard in the rear of the building, where lay the corpse of the old lady, with her throat so entirely cut that, upon an attempt to raise her, the head fell off.*

Tonight was not going to be another occasion for drowning sorrows with red wine and horror stories. This situation was untenable. To produce new life you had to cut back the dead flesh. What the business needed was a sacrifice, a real one this time, and it had to be tonight.

Sidney had killed animals before, slitting their throats and watching the life go out of their eyes, but somehow Sidney always knew it would come to this.

The kit was prepared, lying ready in the bathroom cabinet. Sidney recited a favourite Latin incantation, summoning the strength of Lucifer himself, then dressed in a long leather coat, grabbed the woollen hat lying on the hall table and headed out into the Cornwall night.

What with the restraining order, it would be far too risky to approach the Smyth house without further planning, so it would be Mrs Godbeer who would play the role of the sacrificial flower tonight. In her miserable and confused state, she'd probably thank Sidney for putting her out of her misery.

By the time Sidney entered the house, the whole street was silent. Truro wasn't exactly a late-night type of place. The lock on the back door was an old three lever – not difficult to jimmy open with the lock pick set. Sidney fitted the shoe covers, latex gloves and plastic cap. With no forensic evidence and no clear motive, even Poe's detective C. Auguste Dupin wouldn't have a chance in Hell of solving the case.

Mrs Godbeer's galley kitchen smelled of sweet condensed milk. Sidney shuddered and moved into the carpeted lounge, careful not to displace any of the funeral cards sent by well-wishers. As expected, the old crone was upstairs, and snoring with metronome regularity.

The intruder cast a shadow over the bed like a high priest at the altar on judgement day. *What a pathetic individual. She would have to do.*

'Dark Lord. Let this sacrifice bring renewal, vitality and success.'

Mrs Godbeer stirred, but continued her rhythmic breathing.

Without further hesitation, Sidney wrapped the ends of the florist's wire around specially padded gloves and plunged down upon the throat of the sleeping pensioner with a terrible force. The taut wire sliced deeply into Mrs Godbeer's neck, crushing her windpipe and cutting into the flesh at each side of her neck. For the first time in a long time, Sidney felt in charge, powerful. Death was not something to be feared, but celebrated. Mrs Godbeer didn't even have time to open her eyes. It was over quickly. The old lady's feet jerked up one final time, and then she was still.

According to Poe's manuscript, the head must be completely severed, and so Sidney set about cutting through the tissue with the razor-sharp knife from the sacrifice kit. In order to cut through the spine, Sidney used the strong secateurs. Viscous blood leaked into the mattress of the double bed.

'*Et resurgent meae…. Et resurgent mea,*' said Sidney.

It would be easy enough to dispose of the entire kit in the river on the way home. There were plenty of spares at the shop. The head was finally detached, and it rolled away from Mrs Godbeer's frail body.

As a final touch, Sidney left a single black rose in the glass on the bedside table. It looked perfectly macabre. Poe would have been proud. Of course, the police could trace it back to the shop, but that didn't mean anything. Mrs Godbeer had taken it as a sample after discussing arrangements for her husband's funeral. No evidence, no problem. Sidney left the house via the back door and stole into the night, satisfied with a ritual correctly performed.

* * *

After two months, Sidney had to admit that the sacrifice of Mrs Godbeer had not made a difference to the business. Fran still wasn't returning calls, and that bitch Smyth was still raking it in. Notices from Nairn's Debt Collectors were becoming ever more threatening.

In desperation, Sidney had even used the kit again, this time on an old boar of a man in Chacewater. He was a retired army colonel with a distastefully long moustache. He had said the shop 'legitimised Beelzebub' and should 'sell honest flowers like chrysanthemums and poppies'. No one liked being told how to run their business. The colonel roared when the wire sliced through his leathery neck. Where was his God now? This time, Sidney had planted a neat row of midnight pansies in the front flower bed.

Of course, the police had made enquiries at the shop. A young female officer had taken notes. Yes, Mrs Godbeer had visited the shop and was a lovely old lady. She'd taken a sample of some flowers. Getting the arrangements right for her husband's funeral was a priority. It was important for the business too. Not everyone in Truro supported change. The shop had even had some sarcastic reviews online. The detective had sympathised, and had gone on her way.

The only way to break this run of bad luck was to eliminate the competition. It would have to be a clean job – there would be clear motive this time – but once Black Flowers was the only florist in town again, business would thrive. Fran and Charlie would come back after they saw how wonderful life in Truro could be. They could be a family.

That evening, Sidney prepared another kill kit. This third strike must surely be enough to satisfy the dark powers. All would be right after Prunella was gone. Sidney was doing the Dark Lord's work: cutting back the rotting flesh of society.

Approaching the door of Occasions, Sidney felt a charge of excitement, that familiar thrill of watching their souls leaving their sad bodies. Smyth would be in the flat above the shop, alone. Her husband was away on his weekly trip to Covent Garden Flower market.

Occasions had a well-fitted front door and stout lock, so there was no point in trying to pick it this time. A small pane of glass cracked, then gave way with another two hard elbow blows. Sidney entered and listened for any movement. Nothing. Pollen from the lilies on display choked the air. The padded carpet on the stairs would provide ample cushioning to disguise approaching footsteps.

Sidney nudged open the bedroom door and was surprised to find Prunella Smyth awake, lying in bed with her bedside light on. Even though she was supposed to be asleep by now, it didn't matter. The routine was well practiced – gloves on, cloth for padding and the thin wire. Now that posh trollop could say goodbye to her head.

'What the devil?' Prunella hoisted herself upright. She clutched something under the covers.

'It has to be you,' said Sidney, wrapping the wire around the gloves. 'The others didn't make a difference. He wants your blood.'

Prunella wore a panicked look on her face. She pulled the duvet up to her chest, as if being under the covers would somehow protect her. 'What are you doing here? This is my house, now, now get out. I shall call the—'

'I won't even have a house soon, you bitch. You and your poxy Occasions have taken it away.' Sidney was going to enjoy putting an end to this feud, and hoped that the Dark Lord would be pleased.

'Your Halloween shop makes a mockery of the business,' said Prunella. 'No wonder your customers came to me.'

'And look what happens to them.'

'What... Whatever do you mean?'

'Old Mrs Godbeer was rude about my displays, my black flowers—'

'You mean...? Oh dear God!' Prunella looked frantically for an escape route, but her path to the door was blocked.

'And that colonel in Chasewater too,' said Sidney.

Going into more details wasn't necessary. It was time to put an end to this. With arms outstretched, Sidney sprang forward. Prunella, eyes wide, squirmed to the side and managed to partially block the wire with her forearm. 'Wait!' The pressure opened a gash and blood oozed from the cut. Sidney grunted and lunged forward again. In a desperate attempt to avoid the wire making contact again, Prunella withdrew her right hand from under the covers, and raised a knitting needle in defence. As the wire drew closer, she plunged the sharp end into her assailant's neck. The needle snapped in half and Sidney was left pawing at the foreign object sticking out at a jaunty angle. Sidney staggered backwards, knocking over a vase in the process. Blood gushed from the wound in regular spurts. It must have hit an artery.

Prunella slumped back down onto the bed. It was self-defence. What were you supposed to do when your attacker lay floundering in their own blood on your bedroom floor? The police would believe her, they had to. The restraining order would provide all the backstory they would need. She got out of bed and darted to the opposite side of the room. There was no phone in the bedroom, so she ran to the office down the hall to inform the law. Prunella closed the door on her way out.

As Sidney held the wound and stared up at the ceiling, blood seeped into the beige carpet and stained the fibres a dark red. This wasn't how the story was supposed to end. Smyth had escaped with a minor wound, and it was the wrong florist who was clinging desperately to life.

Fran and Charlie would be sleeping soundly, unaware of the trouble their Sidney was going through to try and get their family life in Truro back on track. A black veil began to draw over the room. They'd come back for the funeral, wouldn't they? Even with everything that had happened, they were family, and it was their duty to look after their loved one. The ceremony would be beautiful: an ebony coffin with white trim and wreaths from the shop – onyx-tinted tulips, and rows and rows of beautiful black dahlias. With eyes now closed, Sidney prepared to make the journey to the underworld.

* * *

The Falmouth Packet, 20th January 2018

BRUTAL MURDER CASES SOLVED

Last night, local resident Sidney Garbrandt was killed after breaking into Occasions, a florist's shop on Truro High Street, and threatening the owner, Mrs Prunella Smyth. Garbrandt, a woman with a history of mental health problems and a criminal record, died from the injuries she sustained in the struggle.

Garbrandt had previously threatened the owner of Occasions, who obtained a restraining order against her. The dispute is thought to stem from the failure of Garbrandt's own florist business, Black Flowers, and her subsequent divorce. Police reported that an initial search of Mrs Garbrandt's property found occult literature and satanic paraphernalia. In addition, the reinforced wire used in the attack is thought to be connected to two ongoing murder cases.

Prunella Smyth, 56, from Truro described the terrifying attack. 'I knew she was dangerous, but we hadn't seen her for months, not since the restraining order came through. I've never been a violent person, but I had to defend myself.'

According to police, Garbrandt is now the prime suspect in two recent brutal murders. The description of weapons provided by Mrs Smyth matches the method employed to decapitate elderly Cornwall residents Daphne Godbeer and Colonel Timothy Manhope.

Henry Winston, Chief Inspector of the Devon and Cornwall Police, issued the following statement: 'Due to the violent nature of the attacks, the investigation had been focused on male suspects, but we are pleased to announce the search for the killer is now at an end. We are satisfied that the perpetrator is the deceased, and we are not looking for anyone else in connection with this investigation. No charges will be brought against Mrs Smyth, who acted in self-defence and notified the police immediately.'

Mrs Garbrandt, 43, is survived by her ex-husband Francis and her young son Charles.

THE VOW

Dänna Wilberg

The weather, unseasonably cold for August, mirrors my deepest need. Here, against my will, I face my destiny.

Upon my arrival, I sign the register, James W. Franklin, as I have done repeatedly in the past. Only this time, I stare at the scrawl of my signature as if I have just signed my own death certificate.

"Welcome back, sir," the desk clerk says. "It's been a while."

"Yes," I reply. "I'd like room 1545."

He balks at my request. "But sir, that room is—"

My deadpan expression squelches further argument. He drops the key into my palm, his hand shaking, his face ghostly white.

Once inside the room, I am surely way past any chance of redemption. I relock the door, toss the key on the bed, and inspect the room, making certain there is no one to witness my insanity. Alone, I listen for her return and I write...

THE VOW

Glimpses of my sordid past are rushing through my brain like a swollen river, flooding my head with the recollection of how this living nightmare began.

I recall my first trip to San Francisco. I was elated at the prospect of becoming a first chair violinist with the symphony – I, a young man from the Valley, obtaining a position normally held only by the most distinguished musicians.

Hard times had befallen many, and the opportunity to earn a living doing what I loved seemed like it was too good to be true. Between the drought and the Great Depression, my family's fortune had dwindled to nil. My grandfather, who taught me to play his handmade violin at an early age, died from influenza, along with my grandmother and three cousins in a short period of time. Music provided solace, and I cherished time alone to wallow in sorrow. But as if grief had not stricken enough, six months later my dear mother joined the others, leaving my father, myself, and three sisters to tend what was left of our meager farm. Life went on, though that which made life worthwhile lie rotting beneath the earth.

One Sunday a stranger drove through our husk of a town. He stopped at our house to ask directions in a heavy German accent. The temperature had risen to 104 degrees that afternoon, so naturally I invited him inside and offered him a cool drink. When he spied my violin on the table, he asked to whom it belonged, admiring its fine workmanship. Thinking nothing of it, I boldly picked up the instrument and began to play. When I had finished he clapped his hands enthusiastically. I am sure my silly grin reflected my embarrassment. No one had ever responded to my playing with such zeal. He asked my age and about my commitment to the farm. I was about to respond when my father appeared in the doorway and the stranger introduced himself as Alfred Hertz, Music Director for the San Francisco Symphony. Mind you, back then we had fallen behind the times, and did not own a Victrola, but I had certainly heard of the man who had recorded the finest music to date. My father took a chair across from the man and asked him if he made a good wage with the symphony. The man confessed the benefits were quite handsome, and my father's face filled with hope. He considered the man a Godsend, and asked him to take me to San Francisco, where my talents could flourish. I was stunned into silence when he told my father he was hoping to do just that. I had turned twenty that year. Alfred Hertz became my mentor, and I, his eager protégé.

I remember the day I arrived at the Palace Hotel clearly, my palms sweaty, my heart beating so thunderously. I felt as though my life were just beginning. As I entered through heavy, ornate doors, I was awestruck by the Garden Court's stained-glass dome and by the Austrian crystal chandeliers. I gravitated toward a mural stretched across the wall in a bar I would later frequent. The Pied Piper of Hamelin *painted by Maxfield Parrish. A beautiful illustration of children being led by a man playing a flute, but where was he taking them? The story's mystery had haunted me even as a child when my mother used to read the tale to me and remind me to always keep my promises. As I studied the mural – again I recall the moment vividly – I was suddenly distracted by the aroma of fresh-baked bread, which turned my thoughts towards sustenance.*

In search of the heavenly scent, and the need to quiet the rumbling in my stomach, I passed brass urns filled with roses, wisteria, peonies, hydrangeas, and more. The colored bouquets and their heady scents made me feel almost giddy.

It was on that glorious day I met Elise. Craning my neck to appreciate the decadence surrounding me, the lowly farm boy, I inadvertently stepped on her foot. Mortified when she cried out in pain, I made matters worse by trying to remove her shoe to inspect the damage. Somehow, my nose got in the way of her indignant response, and she sent me sprawling to the floor, bleeding like an amateur boxer in his first round. When she bent down to offer a handkerchief, her violet eyes clung to mine. Struck mute by her beauty, I managed to stand, my eyes absorbing every delicious detail.

As fate would have it, Elise's father played cello in the symphony, and concluding that our meeting was kismet, I pursued her in earnest. We courted for a year, and on the anniversary of our awkward meeting, I took Elise as my bride, vowing my love for eternity.

We purchased a modest cottage outside the Bay and made a good life for ourselves. I rode the train into the city where I would stay at the Palace Hotel several nights a week during the height of the concert season. Soon Elise was with child and we were deliriously happy – happy, that was, until that one dreadful night when the unexpected happened. Elise went into labor prematurely. By the time the midwife arrived, it was too late. And as much as I hated to leave my wife, the symphony was committed to record live radio performances that week. In order to maintain employment, I had to go, and I left in haste. Even so, I arrived late to the Palace Hotel to find my usual room occupied. I explained my wife's trauma, my dilemma, the sadness, the disappointment, but it was no use. All of the hotel's rooms were filled.

After what seemed like an eternity of my groveling, the clerk offered me room 1545 with the strictest precaution, "Do not open the window at any cost." Rumor had it that people who stayed in 1545 were either cursed or that they went mad. I considered myself above such nonsense and accepted the offer, grateful to have a room at all.

I rode the elevator to the fifteenth floor, anxious to get settled. But as I slipped my key into the lock, a feeling of foreboding shook me to the core. I composed myself momentarily before stepping inside, anticipating the worst. To my surprise, the room was spacious and quite comfortable. I blamed my jitters on our unfortunate loss, tedious travel, and lack of sleep. I wasted no time unpacking my valise and preparing for bed.

I had no sooner pulled back the covers, relishing the prospect of a good night's sleep, when I heard a scratching sound at the window. I drew aside the drapes, mesmerized by the moon dancing on the clouds. I lingered a moment enjoying the view when, suddenly, a young nymph appeared out of nowhere and hovered before me. Her shredded gown accentuated her perfect shape. Red hair fell in waves across the swell of her breast. Dark eyes, like silvery pools, held me in their depths while long nails raked down the glass pane. She pleaded, "Please, I beg of you, let me in."

How on Earth did she end up on the ledge? Ignoring the desk clerk's warning, I unlatched the window and grabbed her hand. Cold as ice, she tumbled into my arms.

"You are kind," she said, shivering against me.

"How did you come to be out there?" I asked, as I grabbed the wool throw from the bed and wrapped it around her bare shoulders.

"I was brought to this room long ago by a man who declared his love for me."

"Did he abandon you?"

"Far worse," she replied, lowering her gaze. "He took something from me I can never reclaim. He made me what I am."

"And yet you return? Why?"

"He made a vow. He promised to be with me until eternity."

"Poor darling," I said, bundling her up and pressing her head against my chest. "I understand such love. I too have made a vow."

Her angst dissolved quickly, and she snuggled in my arms. As I held her body close, a sensation I had never experienced before traveled through my limbs. It felt as though a thousand lifetimes passed between us. Every grain of my existence came alive. My mind reeled and I weakened under her spell. Petal soft lips brushed against mine and the notion to resist never crossed my mind. I had all but forgotten the pleasures of a woman over the last few months. Rendered helpless, my body responded to her touch as she removed my nightshirt and pushed me to the bed. What was left of her garment fell in tatters to the floor and her bare skin shone in the moonlight as if she were made of alabaster. She craved my attention, demanded it. I quickly obliged, not thinking for one moment I was embarking on adultery. My loins ached with anticipation, my mind focused on devouring every inch of her.

At the pinnacle of our lovemaking, I found myself levitating off the bed. Could this really be happening? In my altered state, I sensed her fangs sink into my flesh and I rose to a level of ecstasy that would lead to my ultimate downfall. I could not recall a time when a woman brought me to such fever and I wanted more. With carnal desire, she provided such until early light cast harsh shadows across the bed and I collapsed into a deep sleep. When I awoke, she was gone.

A quick glance in the mirror beside the wash bowl confirmed that my night of lust and deprivation was not a dream. My sickly pallor, dark circles beneath my eyes, and the puncture marks along my jugular didn't compare to the damage ravaging deep inside my soul.

When I returned home, Elise noticed the change in me immediately. Before long, she was rejecting all my amorous advances, claiming I was no longer the gentleman she married, that I had lost tenderness, that I was too forceful, and that my new interests were disturbing. She questioned the love we once had and the vow we made to each other. Arguments ensued. I wanted so badly to confess that I was barely human; instead I moved into another room.

I felt jilted. Elise seemed to blame me for everything from her miscarriage to her lethargy, and her resentment towards me grew daily. I began to stray.

I met my first conquest at a saloon in Heraldsberg, a small town east of the Delta. A lovely thing, she was. We drank whiskey, slow-danced, and then she showed me to her room. *The dank, dark cubicle boasted of a straw tick mattress on a rusted frame and nothing more. She undressed for me, posing seductively beside the bed. "Kiss me," she said. "Kiss me now." I took her in my arms, inhaling her sweetness before tasting her blood. Being it was my first time, I lacked control and nearly sent us both to Hell. From that night forward, I was careful to exercise restraint. If I took a life, it could mean my demise as well.*

My marriage in shambles, I took the liberty of roaming the streets of larger cities at will. My victims, mostly women, fell into my web as if I were a spider. I took precautions, never draining them dry of their blood, never obtaining the thrill I was ultimately seeking. Eventually, I returned home.

After years of heartbreak and torment, Elise relented. She gave herself to me, body and soul. The intimacy we had almost forgotten, now renewed. She proved as insatiable as the nymph in room 1545. And just like the nymph in 1545, when I awoke, she was gone. Elise disappeared as if the curse had come full circle.

But I digress.

Sickened by what I have become, I return to the source. I no longer want to live as a Dhampir – half human, half vampire. She must finish what she started.

And so I wait.

At long last! A scraping at the window causes my heart to leap in wild abandon. Without hesitation, I tear open the drapes. But what I see is not to be believed. The nymph outside the window is another, and more ravishing than the first. In shock and shaking with need, I let her in.

"Where have you been, my love?" she demands in a familiar, deep, sultry voice. "I have missed you so." Her words change to a hiss in my ears. "Do you remember your vow to me?"

"Elise!" I hear myself say, no longer in my right mind.

"Did you think I didn't know about her? About this room?"

"How did—"

Her fingers silence my lips. "My darling, a woman always knows."

I feel the prick of her fangs as I press her body against mine. Heat. Flesh and bone. Euphoria, once again, consumes me. A fire ignites within and I realize she is going too far. "Enough!" I cry, to no avail.

I conclude this account, fading from light into darkness. My hunger is satiated, but life is draining from me. My heart no longer beats. Elise and I will be together once more…

My vow honored – for eternity.

BONES

T. R. Hitchman

Diane stood up with a groan, rubbing that patch of her back that had begun to throb. She had started digging early in the afternoon, spurred on by the early spring sunshine and a sudden desire to do something other than unpacking the mountains of boxes that didn't appear to be disappearing quickly. But even if the weather had been less than ideal, she knew she would have found herself out here. She couldn't quite believe that this was hers. Her own garden.

She had pictured it again that morning in her mind, the overgrown grass and bushes replaced by a well-mowed lawn trimmed with borders filled with the bright colours of delphinium, peonies and hollyhocks. She knew the names of the flowers she wanted; she had even taken to buying gardening magazines lately. There was also a patch she thought would make an ideal vegetable garden. All so different to the concrete and bare backyard of her childhood, and to the little London flat she'd lived in not so long ago where she couldn't even have a window box.

Rob might find it funny if he could see her now, this town girl with her trainers caked with soil and strands of hair limply sticking to her reddening face.

Once they had seen the house, they knew they had to have it. They came across it accidentally. It was Rob who had spotted the 'For Sale' sign and had stopped so abruptly that Diane had lunged forward in her seat, with only the seatbelt preventing her from crashing into the dashboard. They'd called the estate agents' number on the board immediately to arrange a viewing.

The pair of them were all the more taken with it when they stepped inside. It needed work, but it had character and potential, and then there was the garden, which sprawled in front of them full of possibilities. They were like excited children.

'Shall we make an offer, then?' Rob had grinned, holding her hand tighter, and she had nodded, too excited to say a word.

Then, two days before the moving date, Rob had stood awkwardly in the kitchen of their old flat. He bit his lip nervously. His hands were tense as if ready for a fight.

'I've got to go away for work,' he said. 'Ireland, only three days...'

He knew what his wife's reaction would be and she didn't disappoint.

'Christ, Rob... timing! We're moving!' she shouted at him.

Rob had shrugged his shoulders, but he had smiled with a kind of arrogance, knowing that his wife would forgive him eventually, that really there was nothing she could do to change his decision. Diane had sulked to the bedroom, tearful that she knew it too.

But she had managed the moving well enough without him. The removal firm had been very good, and in hindsight there had not been quite as much to deal with as she had supposed there might be. Rob had rung just as she found herself alone in their new home for the first time, with the removal van slowly pulling away from the drive.

'You're in, then?'

She could almost see the relieved smile that grew on his face as she breathlessly told him, 'Yes, but there are boxes everywhere. I don't know where to start.'

But start, of course, she had done, unpacking enough in the way of essentials to prepare food for herself and sleep in a made bed. Now, she stood in the garden, taking in its size once again and thinking about the work that she supposed would need to be done on it in the coming months. She wondered why the couple before had left it so untouched, but this just made her all the more determined to make progress with it. She wanted to impress Rob on his return. His parents had a lovely cottage in the Cotswolds, pretty, the sort you saw on fudge boxes, with roses in summer and looking just as beautiful covered in snow. His mum was particularly green-fingered. Diane would show them that she too could be. What she lacked in experience, she would make up for with enthusiasm, tenacity and Google searches. She had found the spade, along with a variety of other garden tools, in the shed. The lock, brown with rust, broke away more easily than it looked it might, and the items themselves appeared as if they hadn't been used for a great many years. She would clean and oil them, and replace or supplement the items with new as necessary.

She returned to her digging, working solidly for

another half an hour until her spade hit something hard. She grunted as she struggled to dig whatever it was out of the soil. When she had finished, she laid it on the small pathway, which wormed its way from the house cutting the garden into two uneven halves.

It was a bone.

Diane continued to dig. There were more. They came in a variety of sizes and she carefully unearthed each one and placed it on the path next to the others, as though it were a macabre jigsaw. And like a puzzle, she began to arrange the pieces, moving a bone here, placing another one beside it. In the end, Diane went back inside and came out with an empty cardboard box. She carefully filled it with the bones and carried it back inside. Then she covered the kitchen table with a sheet of bubble wrap left over from unpacking and began recreating on the kitchen table what she had begun in the garden.

With apparently four legs, it had to be some kind of animal. Diane had found a fragment of its jaw, some of the teeth still attached, brown and sharp. She discovered how much as one of her fingers caught the edge of a tooth and it quickly began to bleed. She ran it under the tap for a few minutes, wrapping it tightly in what she hoped was a clean tea towel. Then she looked back at what she had created. The animal must have had a huge set of teeth, and her imagination suddenly pictured some strange wild beast. If Rob were here, he would tell her not to be so melodramatic. It was probably a domestic animal, a dog obviously. A well-loved family pet.

Diane recalled Sandie. Mum had bought him as a present for her one Christmas. She had come down to find a box, wrapped clumsily in bright red sparkly paper and then this small, blonde, furry head sticking up and surveying its surroundings with wide, excited eyes. It had been love at first sight, and that dog had been Diane's constant companion through those difficult adolescent years, when he would listen faithfully to her teenage woes of lost love and misunderstandings. She had come home from university to the sad news that he'd had a fit and died in his sleep. They still talked about him now and then when she met with her parents or her sister. So distraught was the whole family on Sandie's death that they never got another dog. No other could replace that faithful and loving member of the family.

Diane took a closer look at the skeleton. It *was* bigger than your usual family dog. She had placed the fragments of its skull at the head of the table and could see that it must have been huge. Perhaps it was a Great Dane or a St Bernard. She looked closer and studied a thin crack that staggered its way deep into the surface of the largest of the skull fragments. Perhaps it was this that had caused the poor animal's demise, and Diane shuddered thinking of the pain it might have been in.

She gathered up the bones and returned them to the box, deciding to give the poor creature an official burial in the morning, perhaps putting it in the sunniest part of the garden. Perhaps she could mark the spot with something that would flower the next spring. With that thought, Diane returned to her spade, working until the sun began to fade and her back could take no more.

Exhausted, she went to bed early, not long after eating. She had eaten sitting on the sofa, not wanting to sit at the kitchen table – she told herself – because she was on her own, but perhaps her decision had more to do with the bones that had only recently been there. As she ate, she regretted not having unpacked the TV yet. It would have been welcome company. The house felt silent and a little strange, and she missed Rob.

Annoyingly, she was just on the verge of falling asleep in bed when he rang. She stayed cheerful, though, telling him in excited tones about the bones she had found in the garden, laughing to hear him tutting comically at her when she described, in her usual dramatic style, her imaginings of the bones being from some monstrous creature.

After the call, which ended with their mutual declarations of love and of missing each other, she soon found herself slipping easily into sleep. However, in the night she awoke with a start. The loud bang made her sit up abruptly and stare wide-eyed into the darkness. Her hand wandered to the empty space where Rob should have been. Was it somebody banging on the door? She crept towards the front window, pulling tentatively at the edge of the curtain. There was nobody there, so she quickly ran back to bed, pulling the duvet protectively around her.

The second knock was louder still; whoever it was certainly wanted to be heard. Diane, now filled with fear, again eased herself out of bed. She stood on the landing. It sounded again. The knock was not at the front at all, but the back. She gripped the bannister, wondering if she should ring Rob, but what could he do all the way away in Ireland?

She stood hesitatingly. Her curious side wanted her to edge forward, the other was like a frightened child pulling her back and it was this that she obeyed. She stood almost motionless, seeming to hold her breath. And she remained there, even when after another few minutes there was silence, as if whoever it was had given up and walked away. When she returned to bed, she wrapped the duvet protectively around herself, cocooned until she eventually fell back asleep.

In the morning, after she had awoken to bright sunshine, it seemed easy to put the knocking down to somebody making a mistake knocking at the door of the wrong house. She went out into the garden, a mug of tea held in her hand, to survey yesterday's hard work; but she almost dropped it in horror when she saw the trail of footprints that snaked their way to her back door. She followed them. They were large and oddly shaped, and – she shook her head at this as the idea seemed ridiculous – whoever it was hadn't been wearing shoes.

She spent the day in the garden, but found she was nervously looking around herself a lot of the time, wondering if she was being watched. She finished earlier than she'd intended, thankful to go inside and shut the door behind her.

Of course, on the phone that evening she told Rob about the knocking in the night. He told her to try not to worry, that he was sure she was right that it was somebody who had got the wrong house. She didn't mention the bare feet footprints; it seemed too ridiculous to put into words.

But that night, again, she was woken by the sound of the knocking. She sat bolt upright and scrunched the edge of the duvet up in her hands, clinging to it like a string of rosary beads. Eventually she went to put her foot out, then changed her mind as soon as it hit the floor, quickly tucking it back into safety. What was the point of going out into the landing, or even worse skulking down the stairs like a cat, only to stand there fearfully? They would go away, presume that nobody was home. But then this thought released a new, unexplored fear. An empty house, perhaps that's what they wanted, some chancer hoping to find an empty house to burgle. The 'Sold' sign was, of course, no longer there. As she was thinking about whether that was a good or a bad thing, the knock came again, so loud this time that Diane was convinced that the door shuddered in the frame with the force. She pulled the duvet tighter, as if this would be any protection against a supposed invader. She thought about how she could arm herself. All she could think of nearby was the vase she'd recently unpacked, a housewarming present from her parents. Could that make for a weapon?

The third knock never came, but the silence that followed was still more torture for Diane. She now waited for the breaking of glass or, perhaps, the loud thud as whoever it was gave the door a good kick. Then she remembered the pattern of shoeless feet that had zigzagged their way across the freshly dug earth. She looked anxiously towards the window, and the hastily drawn curtains, wondering if she could look out and perhaps see a passer-by walking their dog or even a neighbour coming home late, but she resisted the urge to leave the supposed safety of her bed. There was an element of pride too; she had not wanted the neighbourhood to see their new resident hanging out of the window screaming out for help from an imagined ghoul. So, she shivered in the darkness, forcing her eyes shut, hoping that sleep would come soon; but it was a good few hours, or so she supposed, before she drifted off.

Before making herself breakfast, Diane surveyed the back door. Whoever had paid her a nightly visit had certainly thumped the door hard. So hard, in fact, they had cracked the paintwork. She examined it more closely, brushing off flakes with the tips of her fingers. At least it was proof that she wasn't completely crazy, but it made her more than a little frightened too. She cautiously looked up the garden. Perhaps he was hiding behind the shed now. She quickly moved back inside the house, locking the door behind her and checking that it was locked several times before she put the kettle on.

For the rest of the day she felt jittery. She stared out of the bedroom window at the garden. Just a couple of days ago it had been a wonderous place, full of possibilities; now it had become something that she dreaded, and she wondered if she could ever go out in it again on her own.

At least, Rob was due home that evening. She waited eagerly for his return and greeted him over-enthusiastically when he did so, almost knocking him to the ground with a hug, which took him by such surprise that he yelped.

'Well, you must have missed me, then!' Rob pulled her back, but his smile fell a little when he saw the troubled expression on her face.

'Yes... yes I have actually.'

He held her for a moment in silence, then asked, 'What is it? Is it the knocking at the door? Is that it?'

'Yes. So basically,' she replied, letting more of her upset and anger show through, 'some weirdo has been coming into the garden in the middle of the night and knocking at the back door. Really fucking hard. He's hit it so hard it's cracked the paint.'

She led Rob to the back door to show him this, but he seemed so underwhelmed by the evidence that Diane wanted to hit him.

'And he wasn't wearing shoes,' she said and marched

up the garden pointing out the footprints, but somehow by now they had become shapeless blobs and Rob shook his head.

'So, he is coming into the garden, at night, banging on the back door with no shoes on?' Rob was incredulous.

'I wasn't imagining it if that's what you mean,' Diane retorted angrily, seriously annoyed by how lightly Rob was taking all this. 'It was loud, Rob, so loud it woke me up, and two nights running.' She could feel that small vein in her forehead begin to pulsate, the one that always did when she was angry.

'Look… I'm not saying you're making it up…' He reached out and tried to grasp her hand, but she pulled away.

'I know what I fucking well heard, Rob,' she snapped.

Later that evening he attempted to make it up to her by cooking dinner, and Diane appeared to have forgiven him or at least calmed down. They were still recent newlyweds, after all, and any rows that they had never lasted very long.

After they had finished eating, he peered into the cardboard box, the one containing the bones. 'A dog, you say? It must have been a big one,' he said examining one of the bones.

'I'm going to bury them, give the poor animal a bit of a send-off.' He pulled a bit of a face at this. Rob didn't understand about animals; she had told him about Sandie, but she could tell he didn't quite get it. He'd never had a pet whilst growing up. Sometimes she wondered how he would fair if they had children.

Diane had been awake before the knock, which came just as loudly as it had before. This time she snatched Rob's arm, who was already sitting up himself.

'I told you so,' she said, a little bit of her triumphant that she had been proved right, despite the remaining part fearfully wishing that she hadn't been. She held onto his arm.

'That bloody idiot is going to get a piece of my mind,' Rob hissed and quickly threw the duvet back, swerving to miss Diane's outstretched hand.

'Just call the police, Rob. Please don't go down there. It could be some crazy drunk...' But he wasn't listening. He was out in the landing, then swiftly running down the stairs. Diane jumped out of bed herself, then scrambled to find her dressing gown and then hesitated on the first step of the stairs, her foot paused. She felt sick.

'Rob? *Rob?*' But he obviously wasn't listening. The light came on in the kitchen, and Diane shrank back. In the darkness it hadn't seemed real.

She had expected noise, Rob's annoyed voice, whoever it was on the other end. But there had been something like the squeal of a cat, as if a creature had been very frightened indeed. And the silence that followed made her even more fearful, and she nervously placed a foot on the next lower step, forcing herself to take another and then another step downwards until she was at the bottom of the stairs.

'Rob?' Diane hissed, frightened to make her whisper any louder. She walked slowly towards the light of the kitchen. That sound? She wasn't sure if she was imagining it. It sounded like gurgling, as if somebody was choking on something. She wanted to run back up the stairs, get her phone perhaps, but something made her carry on with her journey.

The door of the kitchen was slightly ajar, and all she could see at first was Rob's outstretched hand. It was moving, as though the fingers were trying to take hold of something, but there was nothing there to hold. Then the fingers uncurled and remained that way. Diane moved slowly forward towards the hand... and the sound, the sound of something choking. Closer still, her gaze followed Rob's arm, his shoulder, his naked chest. She couldn't quite understand why he was on the floor.

Diane squinted in the bright light. Her husband lay at her feet, his eyes still open. He stared up at her and there was something innocent about his expression, one of disbelief, that of a lamb in the slaughterhouse. Her eyes wandered further down, and she bit into her tightly clenched fist to stop herself from screaming. A thick gash, glaring up at her like a smile across Rob's stomach, oozing with blood. She fell to her knees and crawled towards him, slipping and sliding in the thick glutinous pool that swelled around her dying husband like a flower in bloom.

Diane stared up at the thing that towered over them both, its body as muscular as a bull, its horns gnarled and twisted, one of them glistening with blood suggesting something unholy. But it appeared uninterested in this woman who now whimpered. With its black and pupil-less eyes it searched the kitchen, before its gaze finally settled on the cardboard box. The cardboard box of bones. And this it howled at.

The sound reverberated, loud enough to be heard several streets away. A man walking home thought it sounded like an animal, a spoilt family pet left out in the dark he supposed. He hurried home, his quickening walk eventually breaking out into a run.

MASTERPIECE

Ian Gough

I t was almost complete. The artist looked to his clock where the fluorescent green glow fuzzed the numbers 2.36am. Hours had melted like minutes. Evening had ticked on into night and night had ticked on into the small hours with him barely noticing, so caught up in his creative surge had he been. The net curtain at the open window swayed a gentle wave as the night breeze, minimal on such a balmy summer's night, touched his arm.

He took a moment to admire his work. Almost complete, he'd savoured every broad stroke, devoured the joy of the finest detail and relished in its vibrant colours crafted into what was to him a masterpiece, unlike any he'd managed before. Yes, he'd painted others, moulded sculptures with clay-covered hands, but this, this was almost perfection, almost. Just another couple of strokes at the edge would bring out the true beauty of the portrait. He called it a portrait, yet it was so much more, capturing the essence of his one true love. It was captivating.

Still, the final verdict was not his to make. Only his beloved who'd supported him since the beginning could be the one. Those sharp-tongued vipers that spat a venomous bile of scathing comments, writing harsh reviews on what they failed to understand as genius, were not worthy of this. They were not even worthy of his thoughts and it annoyed him that they had even crossed his mind. He took some deep breaths to try and restore his calm. The only person that mattered was the one he'd created this for. Mere minutes remained for the last marks to dry; then it would be ready. A swell of eager anticipation rose in his chest.

He paused. Perhaps he should wait to show her it until the golden glow of sunrise. Should he allow her to rest and witness his achievement with fresh morning eyes? Impossible. Buzzing with excitement, he wanted them both to experience the moment together, right now. Besides, the moonlight setting would enhance the richness of tone. No, waiting was out of the question. He had to share his art with the inspiration for his creation now.

He looked down at his T-shirt. Once white, it was covered in paint stains, as were his hands. This wouldn't do. How could he present his composition to the one person that mattered most looking like this?

Removing the T-shirt, he tossed it to the floor. Then he scrubbed his hands in the nearby sink with vigour. Using a harsh pad, he scraped away paint flecks and watched as the rivulets of colour washed away, swirling down the plug hole like rust-infused wine. Red blotches remained upon his fingers, skin aching from hours of toil then scrubbed near to tearing.

Buttoning up a crisp white shirt, he decided on his grey suit, which he kept only for special occasions. If there were any doubt, then his wearing this proved how exceptional the moment was to him. Flattening the jacket lapels, he took a deep breath, satisfied with his mirror image. Decision made, it was time to bring out the light of inspiration responsible for his miraculous masterpiece.

Opening the door to her bedroom, he could see the back of the wheelchair where his darling rested. Golden locks draped over the back support, trailing halfway down the seat. He longed to scoop her up in his arms, yet with the trauma she'd experienced in recent days, he knew his desire must be repressed. So much pain and suffering, and for someone so beautiful. There were days when the strength of his love grew with such power that it hurt.

'Not long now, my love,' he said, approaching the chair and gripping the handles in order to turn her around.

Her limp, almost lifeless body shifted, a slight move to the left. For a brief moment he thought she might slide from her chair and collapse to the floor. No, of course not, how stupid of him. There was no way she could fall; he wouldn't allow it.

As she sat still in semi-consciousness, he laid a piece of folded cloth across her half-closed eyes. He wanted her to experience the full impact of the wonder he had created. To witness her surprise and adoration when she first saw it could only bring him joy. She would understand what her beauty had inspired.

After wheeling her into position near an open window, he slid the net back to allow the faint glow of the moon to fall upon the spot where he planned to display the completed canvas. With care he draped a folded sheet over the portrait, taking steps not to touch or mark his work, before moving it to an easel stand for display. Turning to face his one true love, he knelt and with the most delicate touch rubbed the back of her hand to make sure she was awake. Her patience, to sit and suffer while he crafted the portrait, would so soon be rewarded.

He watched her shudder, hand twitching as fine porcelain-like fingers gripped the arm of the chair. She made an attempt to move, but quickly gave up on the effort as though any resistance would be a waste of what little energy she had left, and her body slumped back in the chair. Once she had stilled, he ensured the firm straps around her wrists and ankles were tightened for her own protection. With all she'd been through, it was the least he could do to prevent her from self-harming. Earlier that day hadn't she already stumbled in an attempt to flee? Yet once again he'd been there to care for her, a guardian knight shielding her from distress. He would not chance that happening again.

'It's alright, my love, you are safe. I woke you as I have completed my portrait. I want you to be the first to see it.'

Her head rocked as he lifted the cloth from over her eyes. It had become stained and damp, so he dropped it to the floor, near his T-shirt, and stepped back as piercing blue eyes focused on him. Smiling, he made a grand gesture, extending a hand toward the easel.

'It's time,' he said, taking care to lift the sheet slowly for the grand reveal.

The artist watched her face for expression as her eyes focused on his creation. As she absorbed the full extent of his work, he hoped that the outpouring of his naked soul was as evident to her as it was to him, that she could understand and truly appreciate his artistic vision. Her reaction was the pivotal point. It would either send him into the upper reaches of elation or destroy every part of his inner being.

'What do you think?' he asked, struggling to contain the excitement. 'Without you none of this would have been possible.'

A tear ran down what remained of the red pulp of flesh on her cheek. She opened her mouth to scream, but the stub where her tongue once was could only gargle a mouthful of her own bitter blood. The portrait possessed so much more than her essence. At its centre was her own lifeless skin, peeled from her skull the previous night by this crazed madman. The portrait stared back at her with hollow black eyes, and in them she saw the depth of this man's evil personified within her own facial features. She moaned, whipping her head to look away from the filth, pulling at the wrist straps to no avail.

'What's wrong?' he asked, now agitated. 'You don't like it do you? I can always add more of you if you think that would bring it to life.'

The artist was devastated. This was supposed to be his glorious masterpiece, yet her reaction was… this! 'Look at it!' he yelled.

Stepping forward, he gripped the gore of her bloodied face, digging his fingers into her jaw, wrenching her towards him until their eyes met. Wrath contorted his features into a vile snarl, and once more she recognised the vicious beast, broken free from its cage, his true nature revealed to her once again.

His words spat out with pure hatred. 'Can't you see I spent the whole night pouring my heart into your own sweet face? How could you be so ungrateful? I've immortalised you and this is how you repay my love!' His hand dropped to the side table next to her chair, a table containing the tray where the large slice of her tongue, torn from her mouth hours earlier, lay soaking in a pool of blood. He grasped the blade that lay beside it, the same one used to carve away her flesh and peel skin from the bloodied tissue beneath. He pointed it towards her throat. She squirmed and tried to push herself away from it, yet her bonds were tight and restricted all but the slightest movement.

'I thought you were the one, but you're just like all the rest. You don't appreciate me or my art. You hate it!' he screamed, wild-eyed.

Lunging, he plunged the blade deep into her stomach, forcing it upward until part of his hand passed into her body. Ribs cracked under the force of the thrust until, convulsing, she coughed out blood onto his arm. Her head fell forward resting against his shoulder. The pulsating rage surged through his body as her life faded.

The artist stepped back, staring at what he'd done. Blood seeped through his cuff, and a pool of it formed below the wheelchair. His fingers loosened and the blade fell to the floor, landing beneath the foot rests of the chair. The hatred behind his eyes slowly melted and the painter, not the artist, re-emerged. His breathing settled back into a more regulated pattern, his heart thumped less and settled back into more controlled beats, and his composure returned.

Perhaps he'd been mistaken all along. Fooled into thinking she was his one true love, when she was nothing more than a distraction. Interrupting his search for the real one who could understand what it took to become a master of his art. Returning to the portrait, he carried it to his own personal gallery and hung it next to his previous works. He'd been so close this time. So close to creating a masterpiece, yet once more thwarted by someone he trusted. Someone who failed to understand what he was trying to achieve.

There was no choice. He needed to seek out a new inspiration.

Tomorrow he would find a new subject to paint.

THE TOY SHOP

Sue Eaton

We have just moved house. I didn't particularly want to come and live here in this village, but I didn't really have any choice about it. And now I need to make the best of it. Perhaps it's not so bad. I like things like plants and nature, and there's plenty of space.

I leave my parents arguing something about the chimney and go exploring again. The garden itself is big, but there's also a half acre field. I take Patch and head for that.

It's summer and the grass is high. Patch runs through the meadow, tail swirling like the rotor blades on a helicopter. At least, *he's* happy. If he could laugh with pure joy, I'm sure he's doing it now. So much freedom. I head for the tree in the top far corner of our field, but when I climb up into the leaves I find what causes me a bit of a dilemma. Inside the foliage, resting on the main branches is a tree house – a tree platform to be precise but somewhere to use as a den. I had been going to use the abandoned stable on the lower edge of the field, but now I have a wonderful hidden spot. Which to use as the main den? I sit on the edge, legs dangling and ponder the complexities of country living.

The sound of Patch barking at me brings me back, so I drop to the ground just behind him, making him spin in a frenzy before sliding down the grassy bank to the old stable. It's then I notice that the fence between the field and the back of the stable has broken down. On either side of the break are a couple of young damson trees and the branches meet over the gap making an inviting doorway. I can clearly see a tall cabbage gone to seed and some potato plants struggling among the weeds. I step through the gap intent on exploring further.

Suddenly, I am not in the vegetable patch. I don't know where I am. My throat is tight with fear and I turn in panic as the door I didn't even know was there shuts behind me with a sharp snick. The leaf pattern in the glass panel is reminiscent of the damson trees arching the gap and I can see the sunshine shafting through, and I sense Patch whining for me. I reach forward, but as I put my hand on the knob I hear a soft shuffle of approach and a light cough as if someone is trying to get my attention.

'Ah, a boy. Just what this shop needs, a boy.'

Mum has always gone on about being suspicious of strangers and this man is stranger than most. He holds out his hand in a gesture of welcome and I recoil. As I do so, I knock against a tub of footballs and two or three of them fall to the floor. As they touch the planks they change shape and bounce every which way, laughing as they do so. I expect his fingers to be bony, the nails long and sharp, but it is only a hand, an old, worn human hand. I find myself staring in both wonder and fright.

'Oh,' he laughs. 'I suppose it's my head. You're scared of my head. There's no need.'

I can't move or answer so just stare, which I know is rude but it's not a sight you see every day.

He doesn't seem to notice but goes on, 'You know how people sometimes have an artificial arm or leg if they lose their own in an accident. Well, I only went and lost my head.' He roars with laughter, only it doesn't reach his eyes – or his mouth. In fact, no part of the head changes expression at all. It looks like a dummy's head stuck on a human body with staring eyes and lips painted in a smile that looks more like a sneer.

He steps forward, and as I have my back to the door, I step to the side away from him. He side-steps me and we do a little dance. I don't know how, but I find myself deep in his shop and he is between me and the door. I stare at him for long seconds before I feel the floor start to shake and the shop begins to fade. The man becomes transparent, his wooden face with the open mouth disappears and his laughter echoes in the distance as I make a run for it. I burst through the door into the dappled sunlight, my dog dancing on his back legs in delight. A digger is rumbling past on its way to the farm up the road and the ground is shaking under its weight. I hardly notice as I run down the narrow path, past the stable, through the garden, and I burst in the back door as if a killer with an axe is chasing me.

'Good grief,' says Mum. 'I was just about to call you for lunch. I need to go to the shops. Will you be alright with your sister?'

'I'll come and help,' I say sitting at the table. I hide my hands beneath the polished wooden board as they are shaking.

'Go and wash your hands. Never mind hiding them. I suppose you've been climbing trees, judging by the state of your clothes.'

I nod and escape upstairs.

I don't go near the stable the next day, and then the next there's a storm and I stay indoors. I try to push my scare to the back of my mind until it becomes a bad dream and I can pretend it never happened.

We settle into a routine in our new neighbourhood, but I do not enter the field again until about a week after the first incident. It's a Saturday and everyone is at home. On my way to the tree house, I see Dad behind the stable examining the brickwork. I drop down through the field and stand on the path watching him until he notices me.

'I thought we might turn this into a garden shed,' he informs me. 'We can grow veggies here,' – he stamps on the weeds – 'and store them in the stable.'

I nod dumbly. He hasn't found himself in a strange shop talking to a man with a wooden head.

'Come here, let me show you,' he says.

I am reluctant. Patch sits rigidly on the path. He doesn't want to go in either. But Dad is in there, so I suppose it's alright. I step through.

There are no weeds, no Dad and no sunshine. I am back inside the shop. I stand for a moment or two, but no strange man with a puppet's head appears. I begin to relax a little and look about me. It's a toy shop, an odd toy shop in that it has odd toys in it. I don't mean old-fashioned toys like in a museum; I mean just odd. The footballs are still there, all back in the tub. They quiver as I touch them as if in anticipation of a game. I see a sailing boat with its sails fluttering as if in a salty breeze I can smell but not feel. Intrigued, I wander in.

It's close and dark inside, and the further in I go the dimmer it becomes. I see a chess board, but it has more than one layer and you have to play up and down as well as across. The pieces seem to be in conversation with each other but stop and turn to stare at me as I walk past. Behind the chess set is a snakes and ladders game with a tank of snakes sleepily watching me looking at them. I brush past the ladders propped against the wall and stare at Mr Potato Head. 'What are you looking at, boy?' I'm sure I heard it and stagger back a step, before turning and racing through the shop knocking into toys as laughter echoes behind me. I slam into the door and turn the knob.

The sun is in my eyes and Dad is kneeling beside me. 'What happened, lad? Did you feel faint?'

I struggle up. I'm lying on the ground beside the straggly potato plants. 'I suppose,' I mutter back before being sick.

The fact that I appear unwell encourages my mum to register us all with the local doctor, who says I need rest and plenty to drink. So, now I can stay away from the stable without having to explain why.

But I am bored, bored with daytime telly, bored with fruit juice and bored with my own company. I am so bored, in fact, that I shall even be glad when school starts again. Even though we've moved, I'm still going back to the same school, thank God, and I'll get to see my friends again.

'Hey, mate,' says Matt on the first day of term, 'you missed a holiday of orgasmic proportion.'

'I'm sure,' I reply sarcastically.

He goes on and on about his holiday in France before asking me, 'How was the move? Boring?'

'Better than I thought,' I say, wondering when and whether to share my secret about the toy shop. 'Why don't you come for a sleepover this weekend? I'll show you my secret hideout.'

He says he'll ask his Mum. I can talk about my experiences over the weekend. If he laughs until he pees himself, I can show him that it's real.

On Friday, Matt's mum gives us a lift to my place after school. She says it's so he didn't have to carry his overnight case about with him all day, but Matt reckons she's just nosey and wanted to see our new house. Mum shows her around, anyway, and then they sit for ages looking at paint colour charts and pictures in magazines and drinking coffee. I show Matt the best way up to the top field and the tree house, but chicken out of telling him about the patch behind the stable. Eventually, Mum calls to say Mrs Tomlinson is going if Matt would like to say goodbye and that tea would be in half an hour – would fish and chips be alright?

The weather the next morning is bad, and we end up staying in watching the television. Mum and Dad go to the DIY store after lunch leaving us with my older sister, who doesn't care if we are still there or not, being far more interested in her iPhone.

As the weather brightens up I take Matt up to the stable by the path. He seems quite taken with it and walks all around it without anything happening.

'Do you think it would make a good base?' I ask him, trying to sound casual.

'I don't like it,' he tells me, pulling a face. 'I got a funny feeling when I walked around the back. Let's go up the tree again.' So we do.

I haven't revealed anything about my experiences with the strange toy shop at all, and I certainly haven't mentioned my faint because that's what girls do in assembly sometimes and the boys all laugh. Sitting in the tree, hidden from view, I ask him to explain his feelings, hoping it can lead to me telling him what I had seen. 'Why didn't you like it?'

'I dunno. I felt like someone was watching me. It was creepy. This is better.'

I leave it there because I suddenly think I'll sound like an idiot if I tell him. I put it off and decide I will tell him that night when we are in bed.

Our English teacher tells us that 'Macbeth hath murdered sleep,' but my money's on two boys on a sleepover. Mum yells upstairs twice for us to settle down and then we hear her footsteps creak on the treads. It's our last chance; we both know that. We bury our heads under the duvets and pretend that it wasn't us, fooling no one of course.

'Let's tell scary stories,' whispers Matt after we are sure she has gone. 'I'll start.' He turns on the torch and holds it under his face to make it grotesque. Matt loves the bizarre.

'No, I have one.' Just my chance and I'm not going to bottle it this time. I twist the truth a little so it doesn't sound like it happened to me and tell myself I will come clean if the response is right. I take the torch and light my face.

'So, this boy goes to stay with his grandparents who had just moved into a very old house in the middle of the country.' There is no murmur, so I carry on. Apart from the bit about grandparents and me making the stable a potting shed, the story is essentially the truth: the move to a house in the country, a boy exploring with his dog and crossing over into a peculiar shop with the strange shopkeeper and odd toys.

'Wow. Was the shop from the past?'

'I don't think so. The toys look all wrong for that. It just felt weird.' There is the longest silence and I suddenly realise what I've said.

'What do you mean, felt?'

I cross my fingers and hope. 'You know how you felt strange when you walked behind the stable? Well, when I did it I was transported to a weird shop and the shock knocked me out.' Silence. 'It was like a nightmare.'

Matt gives me a strange look but appears to take me at my word. 'I felt really weird too. Sick and dizzy. Let's go back tomorrow and see what happens,' he suggests.

I'm not sure I want to but agree anyway. I want to find out more about the shop, and this way I won't be alone.

It is a lovely morning and the early sun gives the old stable a benign look. Patch sits on the path, as he usually does, and looks from one to the other of us. We decide to go in separately in case one of us needs to go for help. It won't do either of us any good if we're both out cold for God knows how long. Matt stands under the damson trees and takes a deep breath. 'I'll go first,' he says, 'and then when I come out you go in. We'll compare notes.' He takes a step through the gap into the patch.

I watch as Matt turns his head as if he is looking at something I can't see. He starts slowly and then gets faster and faster until he is spinning round and round. He drops to the ground and groans.

'What are you two doing?' It's my Dad. He is wearing wellies and carrying a fork. 'Matt? Are you alright?' Matt is laughing fit to pee himself and I feel myself going red with embarrassment.

'Just playing a game, Mr Wardle.' Matt gets up and brushes dead foliage from his jeans.

'As long as you're alright. It's just that Jon fainted in there the other week. I was beginning to wonder if there was anything in there to upset you.'

Matt steps out. 'Are you going to do some digging?'

'Yes, I thought I would plant some potatoes and Brussels before the cold weather sets in. They'll be tasty for Christmas.'

I doubt that any Brussels will ever be tasty at any time, but don't say anything.

Matt pulls at my sleeve and turns his head towards the treehouse. 'We'll play somewhere else, then.' He drags me away. 'Come on, don't dawdle, Wardle,' he says.

He thinks he's funny, but he's not. And I'm furious with him for putting on the dizziness act and basically taking the piss out of me. I sulk at him. We sort of make up later, but I think we're both glad when his mum comes to take him home.

On Sunday afternoon I decide that I'll go back to the shop on my own and bring something from it to prove it's real. I'll take it to school tomorrow and show Matt Tomlinson once and for all. I march up the path and into the patch without stopping. I'm still so cross with Matt I forget about being scared.

The wooden-headed man is standing behind the counter shuffling a pack of cards. The picture cards have eyes that move and the hearts actually beat. I'm impressed.

'It's the shop's boy. Hello, young sir. We thought you'd tired of us.'

'Why can't anyone else see this?' I stand before him, legs apart, arms crossed.

'Why,' – he spreads his arms to encompass the place – 'there's not enough room.'

'There's loads of room. This shop's enormous.' Indeed, it is considerably bigger than the patch it appears to sit on.

'I don't mean this.' He indicates the space. 'I mean this.' He taps his head.

'You're mad,' I snap.

'Perhaps everyone else is mad and I am the only one sane.' He laughs that idiot laugh of his.

'Can I take a toy home with me?'

'Oh, I don't think that would be a very good idea.' He shakes his head until I fear it will roll off. 'Not a good idea at all.'

'Why not?' I snatch at one of the footballs, but it dodges my hand.

'Because I say so.'

'What about a pack of cards? That can't hurt.'

'I said no and I mean no. Were you not taught what that word means?'

He leaves the counter and steps towards me. My courage has started to evaporate in his anger, and I rock back knocking into a stand of bags of marbles that look like eyeballs. I snatch one and stuff it into my pocket as I swing round to face the door. I hear my dad calling – or is it the woodentop? It's my dad, calling me back to our world. I step through and fall to the ground, but I'm alright this time. I pick myself up and run down to the house without a backwards glance. I'll show that Matt.

The bag of marbles appears to have survived its transition from one world to another. They feel hard like marbles but have coloured irises, just like a real eye, and the pupils have widened in fear. I hide them at the bottom of my school bag ready for the morning.

I wake to the disgusting smell of something very, very off. I track it to my school bag and on opening it see that the marbles have rotted during the night and a pool of fetid, glutinous jelly has covered everything in the bottom. My books are ruined and my football kit unwearable. I have the day from hell trying to explain, without an acceptable reason that anyone would believe, why I have no books or kit for football. The cherry on the cake is the detention I have to serve for not being prepared for my lessons.

It is early evening and I stand looking into the vegetable patch. I am fuming but also scared as I was told not to take anything out. One minute I convince myself I was justified, the next I know I was not. Haven't I been punished enough? All my pocket money for the next forever is to go to replace what was spoilt. I am in a right mood. The only good thing to come out of it is that Matt took pity on me and we are friends again.

Due to my grounding, my nan visiting and one thing after another, it's half term before Matt comes to me for a sleepover again. He declares that he wants to believe me but obviously nothing happened when he went in alone. He still admits to feeling odd, though, so is prepared to try again.

Saturday morning finds us standing on the path looking into the vegetable patch. Dad has finished digging it over and the winter potatoes and sprouts are growing nicely in the rich soil. We have come up with the notion that if we hold hands my momentum will take us both through. Matt holds out his hand. 'Come on,' he whispers. 'We'll step in together.'

I count, 'One, two, three,' and fall into the shop. I feel a blinding pain in my left shoulder, like when I broke my arm falling out of a tree. I am on the floor with the woodentop looking down at me. There is no Matt.

'So, the shop's boy is back at last. And still trying it on.' He looks very cross and very scary.

I go to put my hands to the floor to heave myself up and realise that I have no left arm.

'Careless,' snaps the woodentop.

'My arm?'

'Lost it, I suppose, like my head.'

'How?' There's no blood, although I am dizzy with the pain.

'You left it with your friend.'

I can only stare bewildered.

'You were told. There's no room for two boys. I don't know whether I can trust you.'

'Don't worry, I'm not coming back.'

'You're not going anywhere.'

I struggle to get up but can't find purchase on the slippery floor.

'I'll find you an arm.' He disappears into the shop and I think I pass out. I come to as he returns with an arm that looks like it belongs to a shop display dummy.

I panic and try to crawl to the door, but the more I push the further the door seems to be. I collapse breathless and curl into a ball and oblivion. When I come round I find the shopkeeper on his knees in front of me, pushing the arm up through my sleeve, and I hear a click as it slots into place. The pain is dulling into an ache and I automatically try to flex the fingers. They are too stiff to move. I look up at the man and am surprised to see a tear running slowly down his painted cheek. He looks faded and shrunk. He stands. He isn't just faded, he's transparent.

I struggle to my feet. 'What's happening to you?' I demand.

'I'm going home.' The voice sounds very far away.

'No, *I'm* going home,' I am shouting.

'You must wait for your boy.'

I struggle to my feet and step towards him, but he's gone. I turn to the door. The leaf pattern in the glass panel is reminiscent of the damson trees arching the gap, and I can see the sunshine shafting through. I hear my dog whining. I tell myself I can hear Matt calling and see the shadow of my mum joining him. I try to turn the handle, but one hand alone does not seem strong enough and my new hand will not work. Something about the fact that I have to wait for a boy and the age of the man worries me. Did he arrive as a boy? How long did he wait? I find myself feeling drowsy and slip to the floor, curling up against the hard wood. I'll have a little nap and then I'll try the door again.

UPSIDE DOWN

Suzan St Maur

S ilence.
 Then a few creaking sounds.

Then some mooing. Eldred opened his eyes, but saw no cows.

Just the interior of the bus, with crazy trees and plants outside the windows growing from the top down. Rocks pointed downwards, not upwards.

Then the metallic stench of blood, of involuntary bowel motions and fresh urine, of hormone-triggered fear. The mooing became moaning, then gurgling, then crying, then screaming.

Cows don't sound like that unless they're dying. What the hell had happened? Creak, creak. Hot metal contracting in a cool mountain breeze.

Am I dead, thought Eldred? No, because if I'm in Heaven I wouldn't be upside down. I'm not in Hell because I would be burning. A red wave swept over his eyes and he went back to black.

* * *

'Welcome to Alpes-Maritimes,' gushed the guide. 'So happy to have you here for this scenic tour of our glorious mountains, just a few miles inland from the beaches and fun you enjoy at the end of the tour. But *quelle différence, n'est ce pas?* These beautiful scenic sights?'

Eldred thought back to his youth in rural Bedfordshire, England and chuckled. The biggest 'mountain' he remembered from there was the drop from Brogborough Hill in the west of the county – all of a hundred metres or so – before you got to the flat, flat never-ending pancake flatness from there to the east coast of England. No wonder so many airfields were built there during World War Two. And not just because of geographical proximity either.

Eldred smiled as he boarded the bus, having enjoyed a simple and inexpensive flight to Nice to join the tour. I need to do more of these trips now that I'm retired, he thought. Too true. He found his allocated seat, stuffed his carry-on bag under it, and sat down.

'Hello, I'm Pete,' said his next-door neighbour.

'Eldred. Pleased to meet you.'

'Unusual name.'

'My mother loved that name and it has been the bane of my life ever since.'

'Funny, you know. I've heard it before somewhere.'

The two elderly men smiled distantly at each other then buried their noses into their newspapers, a little too indifferent to start a conversation just yet.

* * *

Awake now. No more mooing. No more red waves across the eyes. Much more creaking and screeching. Much more crying, but less screaming.

Can I move? thought Eldred. He tried, and did. He was very bloody. But then so was everyone else. Some were dead. Eldred could see that even from upside down. They didn't move, didn't breathe. Just lay there not even bleeding, because their hearts had stopped.

Over to the right was an upside down window. Broken, shattered. Out I go, thought Eldred.

Struggle, struggle. Pain, pain. But he did it. His world was right side up again. Phew.

* * *

'So why did you come back to Uttersfield?' asked Pete.

'Oh, you know how it is. After so many years out in the wilderness often you feel you should go back to your roots.'

'Never left Uttersfield,' smiled Pete. 'Got a job in a garage when I left school, ended up buying it and running it till I retired last year. Sold it for a good price, I did.'

'Good for you,' said Eldred, trying to mean it. 'I left school early. Moved to America for high school and college then trained as a paramedic. Came back here and worked in the ambulance service in London for years and couldn't stand all the drunks and the fights and the drugs, the violence...'

'So you came back to Uttersfield to get away from the old rat race, eh?' Pete felt self-righteous.

'Rat race? You're right there,' Eldred smiled slightly. 'Not quite what you mean, though.'

By now the bus had climbed way above the Mediterranean, which on this day matched the menacing grey of the clouds. Not your twinkling azure-blue sea today, thought Eldred. Hot, sweaty, humid flat calm.

Roads a little damp and mucky from earlier rain. Evaporation's slow in that humidity.

Still the views were jaw-dropping and they could smell a whiff of lavender and jasmine from the fields of nearby Grasse. It reminded Eldred of his late mum's scent. She always wore it, even to walk him to the school bus stop.

* * *

He was badly cut, but nearly all were just deep scratches.

Thank God my tetanus shots are up to date, thought Eldred. He almost smiled; tetanus was the least of his problems now.

A wave of vertigo hit him like a baseball bat. Flashes of dark London nights. Knife gashes the size of small rift valleys, gaping gunshot wounds made by souped-up starter pistols using home-made bullets. A drunk throwing up a dozen pints of beer and a couple of Vindaloos all over his paramedic partner while trying to fondle her breasts.

Sirens, sirens, sirens. Blue flashing lights. Shouts of orders. People screaming and crying to call more police.

But no. Those were old flashbacks.

This wasn't even a flashback yet.

I can't help any more victims, thought Eldred.

Shame on you, thought Eldred. You've treated thousands. What's another 36, and several will be beyond help anyway?

Eldred vomited, then passed out.

* * *

'Nice scenery, eh?' Pete was beginning to get into a more touristy mood. 'Road's a bit narrow, but I expect the driver knows the place like the back of his hand.'

'I hope so,' said Eldred.

'Yeah, as long as the brakes work proper there shouldn't be any trouble getting this bus around the corners.' Pete smiled broadly. 'Glad it's him driving though, not me, eh?'

'Reminds me of a very tight bend just before you got to my old school in Uttersfield,' said Eldred, almost to himself. 'School bus used to take two goes at getting around it.'

Pete sat up straight. 'Marstonway Secondary Modern?'

'Yes, why?'

'You went to Marstonway?'

'Yes. Did you?'

'Well, of all the... I certainly did. 1961 to 1965. You?'

Eldred hesitated. '1961 to, er, 1963.'

'Hang on a minute,' Pete bristled and sat up even straighter. 'Did you used to call yourself Ed?'

'Yes, until someone in assembly called out my full name.'

Pete was triumphant. 'I *knew* I'd heard that name before. Of course! You were Ellie the Eldred! Well, I never!'

Pete laughed cacophonously, for a long time. Eldred didn't join in.

'I mean, it was such a funny name to us back then, wasn't it?' Pete spluttered. 'We thought it were hilarious, like. Kids. Honestly. Weren't we terrible?'

Pete was still chuckling.

Eldred looked out of the window. It was *that* Pete, after all.

* * *

Flashbacks. Hideous flashbacks. Terror of the gang of sniffling, gurning boys that followed him around the football field at break, sing-songing 'Ellie the Eldred' over and over until his eardrums threatened to implode.

Writing 'Ellie the Eldred' on his notebooks, his textbooks, even an exam paper once.

Snickering with some of the girls, who would sidle up to him and say, 'Want us to show you how to use make-up, Ellie?'

Even raising a smile from a middle-aged teacher who observed the sing-songing and told the boys to be quiet and stop being stupid.

Nobody cared about bullying back then. Not even Mum. Just tell them where to get off, she'd say.

Until, in 1963, Eldred tied himself with a rope to the bannister on the upstairs landing and jumped.

Much to his disappointment, the knot didn't hold. He broke his arm.

And Mum took him to America soon afterwards.

* * *

'No hard feelings, then, Eldred?' Pete still had a half-leer on his ruddy face.

'It was years ago.'

'Yeah, right. You know how kids are. Take the piss out of anything that's a bit different, like. Kids don't understand that you need to be nice to people with funny names or wooden legs or any of that stuff. Or even if they're a bit simple. Eh?'

'So, when did you stop laughing at people's funny names and wooden legs?'

'Oh, you still have to laugh at some of those jokes, don't you? I mean where's everyone's sense of humour gone?'

'Good question.'

'What d'you mean?'

'Do you think people with funny names or wooden legs need to have a sense of humour and laugh at their own funny names or wooden legs because you still think all that's funny?'

'Lost you there, mate. I mean, it's all in good sport, right? Even when we was kids, we didn't mean no harm. It was all just a good laugh. Surely you understand that?'

'Not really, Pete. When kids are that age they don't have the maturity to understand whether people are joking or just being horrible. You and your pals were being, well, horrible.'

'Oh, come on, Elli-Eldred. It was only a bit of fun.'

'Drop the 'Elli' crap, Pete.'

'Surely that doesn't bother you anymore?'

'Not down to you to ask. None of your business. Just don't do it.' Eldred's focus swerved. He listened and looked out of the window. 'By the way, the bus is feeling strange…'

The back of the bus began to slide outwards to the right. On a sharp left-hand bend with a 40-foot drop to its right. The driver braked hard, which was a mistake. The brakes worked too well, because the rear wheels of the bus locked solid.

The bus began to spin, very slowly, and slide. Then, tumble. Spin. Roll over. Roll some more.

There was noise. The high-pitched caterwauling of metal grating metal. The shouts, then screams. The thuds as a 20-ton lump of metal, fibreglass, textiles and humans hit trees and rocks.

Then a few seconds of stillness, silence.

Before the mooing began.

* * *

Eldred wiped the vomit away from his face with what was left of his sleeve. He got up and clambered back to the wreckage, making his way past bodies, stopping to check for pulses and breathing.

A few other walking wounded wandered with him, trying fruitlessly to help.

The driver was dead in his seat, upside down.

A passenger was shouting in bad French down a mobile phone. Finding out where the emergency services where, Eldred hoped.

As many helicopters as you've got, with winches and operators. IVs. Morphine. Saline. Oxygen. Defibrillators. Dressings. Eldred was back in the London Ambulance Service 20 years earlier.

'Elli… Eldred?'

Oh God.

'Eldred, please help me?'

He's still alive.

'I think my leg's bleeding a lot.'

'Can you move it?'

'Yes, only just, though.'

Pete's leg had been impaled by a shaft of twisted metal that had originally been some part of the coach, but which now stuck out from his thigh. A bluish sludge of blood was trying to spurt from it. Cut into the femoral artery, thought Eldred. Got to contain it or he could bleed to death. Can't pull out the metal or he *will* bleed to death.

Eldred ripped the remaining rags of his other sleeve off his shirt, bundled them and applied them next to the protruding metal to block the gash further. He pressed the rags enough to slow the flow.

'Will I make it, Ell... Eldred?'

'Don't know. Depends how soon help arrives and how good their emergency services are here in the mountains.'

'When will help be here?'

'Soon, I expect. Someone was on the phone just now calling.'

'And will you stay with me until help arrives?'

Eldred turned to another walking wounded, who was helping someone to sit up. 'Leave her lying down, for Chrissakes,' he shouted with authority. 'She may have a spinal injury. Just make her comfortable, as flat as possible.'

'You're not pissed off at me about that bullying all those years ago, are you?'

Eldred turned back to Pete and squatted down beside him, still applying pressure to the rags against the metal sticking out from his leg. 'Why do you ask?'

'I need your help now.'

'There's a surprise.'

They could hear the raucous clatter of a helicopter approaching. 'I really didn't mean it all those years ago. We was just being snotty little kids.'

'Fuck you, Pete.'

Eldred reached over and yanked at Pete's leg, pulling it free of the metal shaft impaling it. Arterial blood spurted and gushed like a brownish-bluish-red chocolate fountain.

It was over in seconds.

Eldred smiled.

The helicopter with its team was almost on top of them. At last.

After all, he wasn't much of a paramedic himself these days.

KISSES, SUZI

Joanie Chevalier

C ALCULATING... TURN RIGHT IN EIGHT HUNDRED FEET, JIMMIE.

Jimmie's girlfriend arched her eyebrows. "Since when has your GPS called you by your first name?"

"I know. Personalized service, right?" Jimmie chuckled as his hands deftly spun the wheel to make the right turn. "And you said I was so," – he wiggled his index and middle fingers in an air quote, using his knee to steer – "*old-fashioned* by not using my phone, like everybody else." He feigned pain as Brenda playfully flicked at his upper arm. "It all started when I downloaded the upgrade a few days ago. Listen." Jimmie cleared his throat and pushed a button on his dash-mounted GPS. "Directions to Bob's house."

CALCULATING... HERE ARE THE DIRECTIONS TO YOUR MOM'S HOUSE.

"No, to BOB'S HOUSE... B-O-B," Jimmie articulated, his neck craning toward the device.

CALCULATING... HERE ARE THE DIRECTIONS TO YOUR MOM'S HOUSE, JIMMIE. YOU HAVEN'T VISITED YOUR MOM IN... CALCULATING... SIX WEEKS.

Brenda opened her mouth in surprise, then smirked behind her hand.

"That's never happened before," Jimmie mumbled. He stopped playing with the GPS's buttons when his cell phone rang. He glanced at the screen and groaned. Brenda gave him a questioning look and mouthed, *What?*

"Hi Mom."

"Jimmie, I'm so excited you're coming over," Jimmie's mother crowed through the Bluetooth speaker. "Is Brenda coming too?"

Jimmie looked over to the passenger seat at Brenda, but she shrugged, crossed her eyes, and stuck out her tongue. She wasn't much help.

"Ah, Mom, sorry, we're going to Bob's this afternoon for a barbecue and some football. You remember meeting Bob and his wife once? They live out in the country."

There were a few seconds of stony silence. "Well, *you're* the one who texted me," his mom huffed.

"I didn't text you—" A buzzing noise interrupted him.

"Just as well. I've got to finish up the cookies for the bake sale raffle tomorrow. Goodbye LONG LOST son."

Jimmie grimaced, expecting a loud tirade before his mom hung up, but it didn't come, which meant she was *really* angry.

"You know we've got to visit her soon," said Brenda as she inspected her cuticles.

"Here, check my texts, would you? Why in the world would she think we were coming over?"

Brenda touched her fingertip to the cell's screen and read out loud. "*Mom, I'm coming over to visit. Call me.* And you left two exclamation points."

"What? How in the heck did that text get sent?" Jimmie's brows creased in thought. "Why are you giggling?"

"*You*, texting exclamation points?"

"Yes, exactly my point, thank you very much. What man would, come to think of it?"

"And get this," Brenda continued as she scrolled, "the text was sent only four minutes ago."

They looked at each other.

"Are you thinking—"

"—what I'm thinking?" Brenda finished for him. "Is it a coincidence that your GPS told you to visit your mom and then a text to your mom shows up?"

"Bob's house!" Jimmie said sternly at the GPS, as if it could hear and understand.

Brenda gave Jimmie's cell back to him and held hers up. "Directions to Bob's house," she instructed into it. She looked up and out at the scenery to try and get her bearings as she waited for the directions to download. "Wait, are we going the right way?" Brenda spread her thumb and forefinger on her cell's screen to enlarge the map. "This says we should have turned two miles ago." She brought her cell even closer to her eyes. "Yeah, back at Elm to Highway 50 for six miles."

"Hon, I told you earlier I *just* updated the GPS, remember? It's correct. Just trust me. Suzanne will come around and lead us to the shortest route."

"Suzanne?"

Jimmie's face reddened. "Well, that's what she wants me to call her..."

Brenda shook her head and crossed her arms over her chest. "Oh, I see," she said, her voice clipped. "A machine over me. HER directions over mine!"

"Honey! She's only a machine!"

DING.

Brenda's cell chimed and vibrated so hard it fell out of her hand onto the floor in front of her feet. "Geez!" she mumbled irritably as she reached down to retrieve it, pushing hard against the resistant seatbelt.

Just at that moment, a deer shot out from the left side of the two-lane road and crossed in front of them. Jimmie slammed on the brake to avoid hitting it.

Brenda cried out as the sudden stop caused her head to slam into the glovebox. She sat back up, holding the top of her head with her palm. "Ow, Jimmie!"

"I'm so sorry!" Jimmie said, placing a hand on Brenda's knee. "It was a deer, and—"

"There's already a bump here, Jimmie," Brenda whined as her fingers felt around her head. "Geez, can't you drive more carefully?"

Jimmie knew it wouldn't help to argue that it wasn't his fault. He gingerly felt around the top of Brenda's head as she leaned in closer to him. When she flinched, he knew he'd found the painful spot, obvious by the slowly growing bump. He felt wetness on his fingers and pulled them away.

Brenda's face paled. "Blood! Oh my God... I'm going to get a concussion and die!"

"Honey, honey, calm down! There's no way you'd get a concussion and die just from that. There are napkins in the glovebox. Get one and hold it against your head."

A car horn sounded behind them and Jimmie glanced into the rearview mirror. There were already two cars queued up behind them. He put the car into drive and eased up to speed again.

The first napkin Brenda held against her head was saturated in blood within minutes. Her voice trembled as she retrieved a second. "Maybe I need stitches, Jimmie. Please, can you take me to the nearest hospital?"

Jimmie didn't respond fast enough for Brenda. He was concentrating on getting more space between them and the tailgating vehicle behind them.

"Fine!" Brenda huffed. "Just drop me off at the nearest hospital and you can continue to BOB'S house for a game of FOOTBALL! I'll take a cab home!"

Jimmie sighed. He couldn't argue with this either. Brenda could be full of drama at times, but even he could see all the blood. He pressed the GPS button. "Nearest hospital... Suzanne," Jimmie added, ignoring Brenda's glare.

CALCULATING... THERE IS NO CLINIC OR HOSPITAL WITHIN SIXTY MILES. BOB'S HOUSE IS CLOSER.

"Honey, Suza— the GPS is right. Let's just go to Bob's. You can lie down and relax."

Brenda sighed and leaned her head back on the headrest, now holding a wad of napkins to the top of her head. She closed her eyes.

After a moment of silence, a green road sign flashed in Jimmie's peripheral vision. He was sure it read *Emergency Clinic This Exit*. Even if it *was* the exit, he was going a good eighty miles an hour. He would've had to swerve to make it onto the off ramp, and he'd already irritated the drivers behind him by stopping in the middle of the road a few minutes ago. He could make a U-turn...

No, Brenda will be fine, he thought. *She just needs some rest and a proper bandage.*

Brenda's cell vibrated again. She slowly brought it up to her face and closed one eye to focus on the screen. She suddenly threw the phone at him. "Son of a—!"

Jimmie instinctively threw an arm up and the phone bounced off and flew to the floor again. This time on the driver's side. He clenched his teeth as he pulled over onto the shoulder, abruptly put the car into park, and flung open his door. He paced a few lengths beside the car before he reached in and grabbed Brenda's phone. He scrolled through it and shook his head.

"I don't see anything."

"Yeah, right. You're just saying that to get out of it!" Brenda retorted.

Jimmie walked around to the passenger side of the car and bent over enough to look into the window. Brenda wouldn't look at him, so he opened the passenger door a few inches.

"What'd I do? I was *driving*!"

Brenda continued to lean back against the headrest, but she held out her right arm through the open door and wiggled her fingers. "Give it me and I'll show you!"

Jimmie paced again, this time on the passenger side between the ditch and the car. He kept kicking rocks into the gulley in frustration while Brenda scrolled and mumbled. She had found a clip in her purse and it now held the tissues in place in her hair, since she had to cover her left eye to be able to see out of her right one. It squinted at the cell phone.

Jimmie marched over to the driver side and sunk back

into his seat, slamming his door. He gripped the steering wheel with both hands as if he were about to race in the INDY 500.

"Nothing's here. You erased it!" Brenda pouted.

"Honey! I did no such thing!" He sighed as he twisted in his seat to face her. His eyes widened when he saw her blonde hair was now matted with dried, burgundy-tinted blood, and the side of her face seemed bloated. He tried to hide his revulsion at her appearance and tried even harder to dig deep for compassion. After all, no one had to stay pretty when they were in pain, right?

He tried again. "Brenda, you hit your head. Maybe you were just seeing things. Do you think that's possible?" He had to avert his gaze from her one bloodshot eye staring back at him. He gulped. "Or imagining things? What exactly did you read?"

"It was a text that read *Jimmie's taking me to Barcelona. Hugs, Suzi,* and then four LOL's that were all in capital letters!"

"Barcelona, what? I *don't know* what you're talking about! Barcelona," Jimmie repeated, his voice pitched a little higher than it had been a moment ago. "I would never go on a trip without you, you know that, hon! What—"

"And the next text said, *Look in the trunk if you don't believe me.* What did she mean by that, huh, Jimmie?"

"Hey, hey. Now wait one cotton-pickin' minute," Jimmie said as he held both hands in front of him, palms out, fingers splayed. "First, I don't even know if this text existed, and who in the hell—"

"Oh, so you're calling me a liar, Jimmie?" Brenda interrupted him. It sounded more like a threat than a question.

Jimmie racked his brain for any inkling of something he'd said or lied about before. He couldn't think of a thing.

Instead, he reached over and pulled the trunk release, gesturing to the back of the car. "Go ahead and look if you don't believe me." He kept his lips tight and breathed deeply through his nose a few times. He felt like punching something.

"Really, Jimmie? I'm practically bleeding to death and you want me to walk outside? What if I faint and fall in the culvert? I mean, you didn't have to park so close to it." She made a grumbling noise. "And I can only see out of one eye, if you haven't noticed."

After he got his emotions in check, Jimmie climbed out and walked back to the trunk to close it. He didn't have to look inside. He knew there wouldn't be anything incriminating. He'd never cheated on Brenda. Why would she even think of a thing like that?

But just before he went to push down the trunk lid, he nevertheless took a look inside. There was a colorful brochure in there. He glanced into the car and saw Brenda was still leaning back in her seat, most likely with her eyes closed. He snatched up the brochure to look more closely at it.

What the hell?

It *was* a travel brochure. He jumped as a semi sped past him, whipping his hair around, his khaki's rippling in the draft. In his surprise, he dropped the brochure and it flipped around in the current as if it were a fish caught on the end of a hook. It flopped around and twirled a few times and made one more dramatic loop-de-loop before being carried towards the culvert, where it finally landed out of sight among the tall marsh grass.

Before he could digest this latest development, his cell vibrated. He pulled it out of his pants pocket and squinted at it.

When are you taking me on a trip, Jimmie? Kisses, Suzi.

The text seemed to glow and pulsate as he stared at it. He blinked a few times, feeling like his eyes were filled with sandy grit. As the texted letters grew, his phone vibrated some more and became so hot he couldn't hold it in his hand any longer. He dropped it, shaking his hand in pain. He looked down and saw the screen had cracked and the text *Kisses, Suzi* was frozen on it.

Jimmie wrung his hands, not knowing what to do. No way would Brenda believe anything he said now. How could he explain to her that he didn't know a Suzi? That this person must be texting the wrong number? He shook his head, perplexed. This whole thing made no sense.

He heard the passenger door open. "What are you doing back there, Jimmie? Come on, get me somewhere, dammit!" The door slammed closed again.

Without thinking more about it, Jimmie reached down, grabbed his phone, and chucked it as hard as he could into the tall grass in the field on the other side of the culvert. *The cows can have it*, he thought. The text wouldn't be able to mock him anymore. No lengthy explanation needed.

Who is this Suzi anyway?

When he slid back into the driver's seat, Brenda was quiet, and it was possible she was asleep. *Good, we can make some time*, he thought. Maybe all they needed to do was get to Bob's house. *Brenda will have a chance to relax, drink a glass of wine, and everything will be fine.*

When he gripped the wheel, he cussed and yanked his hand back, examining his palm, seeing the small burn the heated cell phone had left. He put his ear down to it, thinking he was hearing faint popping sounds, like a bowl of cereal after you pour in the milk.

"What's the matter?"

Brenda's raspy voice startled him, and he bonked his head against the driver's side window. He gasped when he looked over at Brenda. She still had the bloody wad of tissues clipped to her hair, resembling a limp red rose tinged with white edges, but she wasn't holding a hand over her left eye any longer. It was bulging and rimmed red, a little ooze of green seeping from the edges of it.

He held a hand over his heart, gasping for breath. Was this someone's idea of a cruel joke? Was he dreaming?

"What's the matter, darling? You look like you've seen a ghost." Brenda stretched her arms out straight in front of her and then her legs. "Wow. Thanks for letting me take a little catnap, hon. I needed that. I feel so much better."

"But... but..."

"Cat got your tongue?" Brenda giggled, now fully energized. "You're so cute, but you knew that, right?" She reached for her handbag and rifled through it. "I'm just going to spruce up and we'll head on over to Bob's, 'kay my little pumpkin?"

She pulled out a tube of Juicy Smackin' Red, one of her favorite lipsticks. Before she had a chance to flip down the visor and open the lighted mirror, Jimmie lunged forward.

"No!"

The only thing he thought of doing to distract Brenda from looking into the mirror was to kiss her. He couldn't bring himself to kiss her with any passion, though, just enough to distract her. He squeezed his eyes closed as hard as he could so he wouldn't have to look at her pus-filled eye. He kept his lips together as well, thinking about that green ooze. The faint smell of a rusty copper penny assaulted his nose from the crusty, clotted blood on her scalp. He was careful to keep his arm and hand on the back of the seat and not anywhere near her head so he wouldn't accidentally touch it.

It was the longest twenty seconds of his life, but was it wrong of him to try and protect his girlfriend from seeing herself in this condition?

Or maybe her grotesque appearance was only in his imagination... He couldn't be sure of anything now. This day was only getting more bizarre. He just wanted it to end.

He grabbed the lipstick from her fingers before she had fully recovered from his unexpected kiss, opened his door and threw it out, far enough for it to bounce across to the other side of the two-lane road. He then scowled and roughly wiped his lips with the sleeve of his shirt, trying to get the smell and taste of her off his lips.

"That was my favorite lipstick," Brenda complained, surprised by his sudden move, but not noticing his apparent disgust.

He ignored her, turned the key in the ignition, and pushed the GPS button. "The nearest hospital." He pulled out onto the road, now empty of vehicles. It was almost dusk, too late for the five o'clock football game now.

Time to step up and be a man now, he told himself. Brenda really needed to be looked at by a doctor. Maybe she *did* have a concussion or was hemorrhaging.

CALCULATING... HE NEVER LIKED YOUR KISSES, BRENDA. HE SAID YOU KISS LIKE A DEAD FISH... CALCULATING... HOSPITAL FIFTEEN MILES.

"What the hell is going on, Jimmie?"

There was no point in answering her. He didn't know himself. He kept driving, determined to get to the hospital now. Maybe once they were there, everything would be all right.

"Hon, you're really scaring me. Why are you driving so fast?"

CALCULATING... HE DOESN'T REALLY LOVE YOU, BRENDA... HE LOVES ME... CALCULATING... TURN RIGHT NEXT BLOCK.

The Ford's tires squealed as he yanked the wheel at the next block. They began climbing, and within a few minutes there were more trees than houses. He looked down the ravine and saw boulders and a creek.

"Jimmie, please tell me what's going on. Why are you doing this?" Brenda's voice trembled, and her hands tightly gripped the arm rests, her back rigid against the seat.

CALCULATING... HE WANTS TO LEAVE YOU, BRENDA... CALCULATING... NEXT LEFT AND YOUR TRIP WILL END.

The left turn came fast and Jimmie barely made it, the tires running over some brush on the side of the road, inches from the steep crag. They jolted as Jimmie ran over a large rock and the glovebox popped open. Brenda cried in pain as something heavy fell out.

"My toe! Oh my God, my toe's broken!"

She violently unbuckled her seatbelt and reached down to retrieve the item: Jimmie's gun.

"You know what?' she said, breathing hard. "I'm going to shoot your damn GPS! That'll shut her up!"

She pointed the gun at the dash.

"Brenda, no! Give me that." Jimmie grabbed the gun from her and began wiping the handle with the end of his shirt. He didn't want to touch her dried blood, sweat, pus, and who knew what else was on her hands. Just thinking about it brought bile burning up to the back of his throat.

"Watch out!" Brenda screamed.

Jimmie slammed on the brake and the car skidded sideways a few feet. The back tire slid over the edge of the dirt road. They were leaning two hundred feet above the creek and boulders now.

"NOOOO!" Jimmie screamed, his frustration level reaching its limit. He gripped the gun with both hands and pulled the trigger, aiming straight at the GPS. After the shot, he covered his ears, which were ringing in pain from the reverberation. The car was tilted to the right, so he leaned toward the driver's door and gunned it. Not touching the ground, the back wheel only spun. Dirt flew, and the car lurched. It didn't go straight, however, but swung to the right. They were now in even more danger of careening over the edge of the rock face.

"Don't worry, honey, I'll get us—" Jimmie stopped, horrified, his eyes glued to the hole in Brenda's forehead. "What the—?"

He heard a click that sounded like door locks disengaging and Brenda's door flew open. Jimmie instinctively grabbed Brenda's foot as her body sagged backwards out of the door, hanging over the precipice.

He groaned as he watched his gun slide down the seat and then drop out the door. He frantically tried pulling at her leg to get Brenda back into the car, but he felt it rock around him, like it would tip over at any second. His hand tingled, and when he looked down he saw hundreds of maggots crawling down Brenda's leg and foot and onto his hand.

He screamed and released his grip, face contorted in revulsion, shuddering every time he heard the snapping of branches and thuds of Brenda's body tumbling and slamming against the cliff wall all the way down to the bottom of the canyon. No way in hell was she alive now.

Beads of sweat rolled down his forehead. He could barely breathe, but found the breath to scream again as the car settled with a screech.

He let out a few shaky puffs of breath and slowly leaned left again, foot punching the gas pedal. The tires whined, and gravel flew as the car wavered.

"Come on!" Jimmie urged as the car began to inch its way back onto solid ground. The engine roared, and he smelled burnt rubber when the car finally got back on solid ground.

Breathing hard, his heart fluttering, Jimmie flung open his door and stumbled to the cliff's edge. He peered down through the trees and boulders, but couldn't see any sign of Brenda. She must be at the bottom.

His shirt now drenched with sweat, he paced, gulping noisily. His mouth was so dry. He didn't know what to do. Call the police?

Then he thought of the hole in the middle of Brenda's forehead. There hadn't even been any blood. He squinted, rubbing his forehead trying to figure out what had just happened.

"Are you in trouble, man?"

He jumped and spun around. Behind him stood an older man wearing hiking attire and carrying a walking stick. An old black dog waited beside him.

"Did you lose the trail?"

"Uh, no, I..."

The man stared at him while his dog sniffed the air.

"I... I was just enjoying the view."

He didn't know why he said it. Now that he'd had a few minutes to think, saying that his girlfriend had a hole in her head and had just fallen to her death didn't sound right. It sounded almost like... like *he* had killed her.

"Well, buddy, the trail is right over there. Loops around on the other side of this ravine. Some like to go the long way." The man pointed out over the ravine and down into it, right where Brenda had fallen. "But then it's a good steep climb back up, and Billy here is too old to do that anymore." He chuckled as he rubbed the dog's ears.

Jimmie didn't know what to say. His mind was reeling with the realization that he was the only one who knew Brenda was dead. He forced his lips to stretch, hoping the old man would interpret the motion as a smile. "Well, maybe next time."

"Okay, well, gotta head home. It's getting dark. No need to be out here after dark." The man pointed to the edge of the cliff. "Be careful now. Cars have been known to fly right over." He shook his head. "Usually teenaged drivers, and then their parents end up having to spend a fortune hiring heavy-duty tow trucks to pull them out." He waved and continued walking on, calling a "Goodnight" over his shoulder.

Jimmie rushed to his car and slammed the door behind him. He took a few quavering breaths, eventually deciding to just get back home. There, he could think about what he should do next. Yes, he thought. The safety of home felt like a good plan.

His hands shook as he turned the ignition. As he carefully drove back to the highway, he heard a voice projecting out of his radio's speakers.

CALCULATING... NOW, JIMMIE, WHO DO YOU LOVE?... CALCULATING.

Jimmie gripped the wheel so tightly his fingernails turned white. "What do you want from me, DAMMIT! What do you want!"

CALCULATING... I WANT ALL OF YOU, JIMMIE... CALCULATING.

"Son of a bitch!" Jimmie yelled as he pounded a fist against the dash. He began to bend the already mangled GPS, furiously clawing at it with his fingers, the sharp edges of the plastic cutting into his fingertips.

CALCULATING... DO NOT CHEAT ON ME AGAIN, JIMMIE... CALCULATING.

He powered his seat back and pulled a leg up and out, transferring his left foot to the gas pedal as he began bashing his right foot against the radio and what was left of the GPS.

CALCULATING... WE BELONG TOGETHER... CALCULATING.

Jimmie was crying, desperate to get away from the voice.

CALCULATING... AS LONG AS YOU STAY TRUE TO ME, I WILL GET RID OF THE EVIDENCE THAT WILL PROVE YOU KILLED BRENDA... CALCULATING.

"I DID NOT KILL BRENDA!" he screamed, enunciating each word slowly and separately. "YOU DID! The... the bullet must have ricocheted off the GPS. Went into her... her forehead." Jimmie wiped at the snot and tears flowing down his face with his sleeve. "It's YOUR fault!"

CALCULATING... WHAT GPS, JIMMIE?... CALCULATING.

Jimmie blinked rapidly. It was now dark and he could barely see the road, let alone the inside of his car. He turned on the dim dome light, looking at the dash where the GPS sat, but there was nothing there. He had shot at it, and then kicked at it, but surely there'd be fragments scattered throughout the car or on the seat?

Frantically searching the seat and the floor with his hand, Jimmie didn't notice he'd swerved into the opposite lane until an oncoming driver blinked his car's headlights and leaned on the horn. He jerked the wheel to get back into his lane, shielding his eyes from the blinding headlights as the car zoomed past. He was only three blocks from home, but he slammed to a stop at the curb, frantic to prove himself wrong.

There's got to be pieces of the GPS here somewhere, evidence that I did not kill Brenda.

The car's interior light flickered, then went out as the car died. He turned the key over and over again, but there was nothing. His battery was dead.

Jimmie picked up his head from the steering wheel when he heard the rolling growl of thunder, a flash of light streaking through the sky in the distance. Fat drops of water quickly turned into a deluge that violently pounded against the windshield. He opened the door and got out, uncertain as to whether he should try to get help or just run home.

Instinct kicked his body into survival mode, and Jimmie began jogging. His feet were wet within his first few steps, and since there were only a few street lamps spattered about to light his way, he splashed through puddles all the way home.

He finally reached his house, clothes sodden and heavy from the rainstorm, hair plastered to his head. His hand shook as he tried to insert the key into the front door's lock. It went in on the third attempt, and he turned the key. A few more steps and he was inside. Leaning back against the door in the dark, relieved that he had made it, Jimmie listened and glanced around, breathing hard from the exertion of the three-block jog and the adrenaline still lacing through him.

Then he jumped, startled almost to the point of convulsing. He started wailing, knees giving out as he slumped to the floor. He placed his hands over his ears to drown out the loud booming voice coming from the living room speakers.

CALCULATING... I LOVE YOU, JIMMIE...
   CALCULA... I LOVE YOU, JI...
   C... I LOVE YO...
   ... I ...

Jimmie didn't notice through his misery that a frayed wire from the stereo set had inched its way from behind the couch toward the water dripping from his clothes and pooling beneath him.

In the next instant, sparks spat and popped around him.

CALCULATING... WE ARE AS ONE NOW, JIMMIE... KISSES, SUZI.

THE MONSTER

William Quincy Belle

"There's a monster under my bed!"

Julie pulled the blanket up to her chin, her gaze darting around in the darkness. She held her breath, listening. Did something move? Was that a scratching noise under the bed? She took a breath, leaning over to the bedside table and picking up her flashlight. She pointed it at the floor and moved the beam of light around, inspecting the left side of her bed.

Julie scooted to the opposite side and twisted so her head and arm hung over the edge. She moved the flashlight around again.

"Mommy!"

Julie moved into the middle of the bed and lay back on her pillow. She held the flashlight straight up, staring at the circle of light on the ceiling. What was she going to do? There was no doubt she would be eaten alive.

"Mom!"

She turned off the light and lay still. Maybe if she didn't move, the monster wouldn't know she was here and wouldn't eat her. That seemed like a good idea. It was worth trying.

The intercom on the bedside table clicked on, crackling with static. Her mother's voice came out, somewhat distorted. "Julie, you have to go to sleep."

"There's a monster in here. I can hear him."

Julie waited in the darkness. Would her mother believe her – would she come down to see for herself?

"Julie...?" Her mother's voice trailed off.

"Yes?"

"I want you to go to sleep."

"Aw, Mom," she said. "I'm not tired. Do I have to?"

The intercom made a few more clicks. "I'm going to let your father talk to you."

Julie rolled her eyes. So much for that idea. Mom wouldn't come and search for her monster. She was going to let her fend for herself.

Her father's voice boomed from the intercom in a deep baritone. "I thought we had a deal, young lady."

Julie lay there, not saying anything. She stared at the ceiling, looking at the shadows cast by the lights from the street.

"Julie?"

Oh boy, was Dad angry? She sighed. "Yes, Dad."

"Didn't we have a deal?"

"Yes, Dad."

"And what was that deal?"

"Two stories then lights out."

The intercom clicked, and she heard her dad clear his throat. "And how many stories did I read to you tonight?"

"Two." Julie shook her head. Why was Dad so logical? With a little protesting, she could get Mom to come to her room. Instead of talking about a monster, she should have said she had an upset stomach. An upset stomach or a headache guaranteed her mom would come look in on her.

Julie rolled her eyes again. This wasn't working. Well, it wasn't working with her dad at least. "You read me two stories, and I go to sleep."

"Didn't you agree?"

She sighed. "Yes, Dad."

"Did I read you two stories?"

"Yes, Dad." Now she was sorry she had ever brought this up.

"Have you gone to sleep?"

"No, Dad."

"I read you two stories, and you go to sleep. I did my half of the deal. Now, we need you to do your half."

"Yes, Dad." Why did Julie bother? As soon as Mom called Dad into the conversation, it was over.

"Now, princess, how about you put your flashlight away and go to sleep?" A couple of clicks sounded from the intercom. "What day is tomorrow?"

"Saturday?"

"Daddy has to go pick up the car from the garage. Everything is all fixed now, and I thought the two of us could go out for breakfast."

Julie's eyes lit up. "Pancakes!"

"Right you are. Now the sooner you get to sleep, the sooner you wake up. And the sooner you wake up, the sooner we get the car. And the sooner we get the car..."

Julie stood her flashlight on its end on the bedside table. "Okay, Dad. I'll go to sleep now."

"That's my girl." The intercom clicked one last time, then fell silent.

Julie put her head down on her pillow and shut her eyes.

* * *

Freddy had been doing break-and-enters for almost a year now. He wasn't getting rich, but he did make a few good bucks now and again. The biggest problem was fencing stuff afterward, but thank God for Old Man Spencer, who ran the pawn shop downtown. Freddy had discovered, by chance, Spencer also did shady deals on the side. Whatever he came in with, Old Man Spencer was willing to take it off his hands. This made things a heck of a lot easier for Freddy, and lately, Spencer had been giving him tips.

Until recently, he had been driving around, scouting out places to hit and trying to guess if dark houses meant the owners were out for the evening or gone on vacation. Once, Freddy found out the hard way a dark home could mean the owners went to bed early. The man had woken with a yelp, scaring the hell out of Freddy. Fortunately, in the darkness and confusion, the guy never got a good look at him, but Freddy made sure from then on to double-check the garage for cars. And even then, if he had the slightest suspicion, he would ring the doorbell several times.

Tonight, Spencer had put him onto a house on Forty-Second Avenue, number thirty-five. He had no idea how Spencer knew this, but Spencer claimed the owners were away for a week-long vacation. This seemed like the perfect opportunity.

Freddy pulled up to the corner, looking for the street sign. The branches of a willow tree on the corner lot swept partway over the sidewalk, hanging in front of the street sign. He twisted his head and saw the number forty-two. This was it.

For the briefest of moments, Freddy tried to remember the layout of the city's roads. Streets ran east and west while avenues went north and south. Spencer had warned him to pay attention and make sure he was on Forty-Second Avenue and not Forty-Second Street. No matter, now. He turned left and idled down the street, looking at the number on the front of each house. Freddy saw number thirty-five and pulled over to the curb. He put the car in park and shut off the engine. The house didn't look like he'd expected. Spencer had said it was a split-level, but this looked more like a bungalow. Freddy thought it sounded odd, but it was time to get to work.

He reached into the glove compartment and retrieved a screwdriver. Sometimes he needed to pry things open, so he liked to be prepared. He got out of the car and squeezed the door shut. A quick scan of the area told him he was alone.

Freddy crossed the street, walked up the driveway, and skirted around back. The light through the garage window was dim, so he took a small pocket flashlight out and shone it through the glass. The beam fell on an empty floor. No cars, as Spencer described. Things were looking up.

The old man had said the best way to get in the house was through a bedroom window, so he picked up a plastic lawn chair as he crossed the back patio and carried it around to the side. He placed the chair in front of a window, glancing between the neighboring houses. The house opposite didn't have any windows on the end wall, reassuring him nobody would look out and discover him breaking in. This job would be free and clear.

Freddy got up on the chair and examined the window. It had a screen he could remove, and the interior window was left open. Somebody must have been airing the room out and forgotten to close it. He used the end of the screwdriver to pop the metal frame out of its supporting grooves and lowered the screen to the ground. He put one hand on the underside of the window and slid it open as much as possible. The gap was wide enough for him. He put his screwdriver in a back pocket, placed both hands on the inside of the sill, and hoisted himself up. Maintaining balance was a struggle, but he got one knee onto the ledge and twisted himself around. He lowered one foot to the bedroom floor and brought in his other leg before standing up.

Freddy glanced around, trying to get his bearings. Spencer had given him the layout, along with a list of items he should look for. The woman had jewelry, the man expensive watches. He took a step toward the hallway when a light in the room came on. He froze.

"Are you the monster from under my bed?"

He heard the little girl's voice and felt his pulse quicken. Something had gone wrong: the family was home. And Spencer hadn't said anything about kids. An older couple owned the house. Were they babysitting grandchildren? What was he going to do now? Jump out the window?

"You don't look like a monster."

His mind raced. What to do? Escape seemed like the correct course of action, but the little girl's voice sounded odd. What was she babbling about? He pivoted. The lamp on the side table cast a dull light over a young girl in bed, her head propped up on a pillow. She stared at him.

"Mommy thinks I shouldn't be afraid."

Her eyes were oddly large, wide open and round. They gave her a look of innocence, but they were also hypnotic. He couldn't look away.

"Don't worry, little girl," he said. "I've made a mistake. I think I'll run along."

The girl looked at him without blinking. "Mommy thinks I should deal with the monsters myself."

This was weird, and he wanted to get out of there. "I'll be going now."

Something gooey splattered across his face. Freddy was so surprised he inhaled. He felt light-headed and unsteady, his strength draining out of his body. He stood there, transfixed, unsure of his surroundings.

Freddy stumbled back a step and dropped to his knees. His energy was gone, leaving him limp. He fell backward and slumped against the wall, his legs stretched out in front of him. Freddy could feel his body, but he no longer had any control over it. He couldn't move his limbs. His mouth hung open, yet he couldn't talk. His eyes darted back and forth in alarm.

He heard the covers on the bed being pulled aside and his gaze fell on the little girl as she rose off the bed. He couldn't comprehend what he saw: the torso of the girl blended into a snake's body, a large one. It uncoiled from the bed as the girl's chest floated over the floor, stopping a few feet in front of him.

"Yes, I should deal with the monsters myself."

He tried to scream, but no sound came out of his mouth. When he tried to raise his arm to defend himself, it lay there motionless. Had he walked into a nightmare?

The girl's torso reached his feet. Paralyzed by her venom, Freddy stared at her, scared witless and trying to comprehend how this snake creature could exist. Her elongated body shifted position, the upper body now lying chest-down on the floor. The little girl looked up at him as her mouth opened. Something changed on either side of her head, and the gap between her jaws grew. He saw something moving under the skin on each side of her head as her mouth opened wide – unnaturally, horrifyingly wide. He screamed silently. But his panic could only echo through his mind as he lay immobilized, defenseless.

The little girl's head was distorted as her mouth became a gaping hole. Her arms seized both of his ankles. They lifted his legs, and Freddy could only watch as his feet disappeared into the girl's mouth. Her torso continued to inch forward in spurts, her arms and hands holding up parts of his body to better swallow. He looked on in utter horror as his calves, knees, and thighs disappeared into her distended mouth. Her saucer-like eyes that perched over the cavernous opening stared into his. As the little girl moved forward to swallow him whole, she never broke her gaze.

When her mouth reached his waist, her tiny hands grabbed hold of his chest, sliding him toward her open maw. His body shifted until his torso was flat on the floor, his head propped up against the wall. The girl swallowed his hips. Her little hands gripped his wrists, positioning his arms against his sides as her mouth slid over his chest. She was now up to his shoulders. Freddy felt her lips around his neck. There was a pause, then the mouth stretched and, with one final lunge, closed around his head.

* * *

Julie returned to her bed, reaching down to draw her blankets up under her chin.

The intercom clicked a couple of times, and a woman's sleepy voice spoke. "Are you okay, Julie?"

"I was dealing with a monster, Mommy."

"Oh, Julie, you had a dream. Go back to sleep."

The intercom clicked, and the room was silent. Julie shut her eyes and fell asleep.

A DARK REFLECTION

Mark A. Smart

DAY 1

I'm watching you. I'll always be watching you. I'll watch when you're sleeping, when you're awake, when you dress, when you undress. I'll even be watching when you make love. I'll always be here. Always watching. Never to touch. Never to be with you.

Kayla shuddered. Austin noticed the sudden shivering movement.

'You alright, babe?' he asked, about to turn his bedside light on.

She looked at her phone in a stand on her bedside table, the screen glowing a subdued green. The display told her it was ten minutes to one. 'Yeah,' she replied, 'just one of those weird feelings. You know, like when people say "someone just walked over my grave."'

'Come here, silly, let me warm you up.'

Kayla snuggled back up to Austin and he wrapped his arm around her as they tried to fall back to sleep.

I love you Kayla.

'Love you too, Austin.'

Austin was already snoring.

* * *

Kayla woke feeling like she hadn't slept at all. She rolled over and put her arm around Austin.

'What time is it?' he mumbled.

Kayla rolled back over and looked at her phone. 'Just gone quarter past six,' she replied. 'Only feels like half an hour since we went to bed. I feel rubbish.'

'Jump in the shower, sweetheart. I'll get some coffee on the go.' Austin flung back the duvet and got out of bed. 'Everything seems better after a cup of strong coffee.' After a stretch and a groan of satisfaction, he shook his head as if to shake off the last of the tiredness still encroaching on his consciousness, then left the bedroom.

Kayla listened as Austin shuffled down the hall to the kitchen. She lay watching the ceiling and listening as her boyfriend rattled around in the kitchen of the spacious ground floor flat she rented. Cupboard doors were opened and closed, water flowed from tap to kettle, and a cat wail preceded Austin complaining, 'Bloody cat, stop getting under my feet!'

Kayla grimaced and climbed out of bed. 'Leave Ferdy alone,' she called. 'He's getting old.'

'He'll be getting dead if he keeps tripping me up!'

Frowning, Kayla went into the en-suite bathroom and turned on the shower. She looked at herself in the mirror. There were dark circles under her eyes. Staring at her reflection like this, it felt like the tiredness were attacking her. The mirror seemed to take on the appearance of silver smoke eddying toward the centre where it started to form the shape of a face. Kayla could do nothing but stare as a pair of eyes formed over her own reflection. A nose began to form, followed by a mouth. She was helplessly drawn to what was happening in front of her, unable to look away but also sure that what she was seeing was only a figment of her imagination, the product of a tired mind.

A sudden loud crashing noise brought her back to reality and she spun around to look through the bathroom door back into the bedroom. She started to shiver. *Had the heating gone off?* she thought. Plumes of vapour formed when she breathed. She walked back through to the bedroom to discover the cause of the noise. A vase of flowers had been knocked from the chest of drawers and were strewn across the bedroom floor, the vase now a collection of glistening shards of clear glass.

'What have you done, Ferdinand?' she called, as the cat attempted a stealthy departure from the room. Kayla looked at the largest of the broken pieces and could see her own faint reflection stretching around the curvature like a bizarre caricature, and then the same swirling mist started forming on the piece she was focusing on.

'You okay, babe?' Austin asked as he entered the room, a cup of coffee in each hand.

The sudden and unexpected question made Kayla jump and emit a short, high-pitched scream before exclaiming, 'Austin, you idiot. You frightened the life out of me!' She grabbed a pillow from the bed and threw it in his direction.

'Woah,' he said, 'I'm carrying coffee here!'

'That's why I made sure I missed,' Kayla replied, grinning. 'Now, be a good boyfriend and clear up this mess. I still have to shower and get to work.'

Austin placed the coffee on the bedside table nearest to him, stood to attention and saluted. 'Yes ma'am. Consider it done, ma'am!'

Kayla laughed and grabbed her dressing gown. 'Idiot,' she said as she passed him to go back into the bathroom.

DAY 2

I've been watching you for a long time. Since that first day at university. You were on a different course, but I noticed you at lunchtime in the refectory. You didn't even see me, but God, I noticed you. It was instant. That feeling. I couldn't describe it. I used to follow you at a distance, watch other lads try it on, watch you turn them down. I knew you were waiting for me, but I didn't have the guts to approach you. Sometimes I'd sit on a bench outside the halls of residence. I'd sit and stare at your window. If anyone asked me what I was doing, I'd tell them I was stargazing, waiting for poetic inspiration. Hey, why not? It was university. Nothing sounds too weird at uni.

Kayla woke and sat bolt upright, gasping for breath. A cold sweat started to run down her brow. Austin murmured something unintelligible before rolling over to face her, slowly rousing from his slumber.

'Shit, Kay, are you okay? You took all the duvet... again. It's bloody freezing in here.'

Kayla's face wore a thousand-yard stare, not focusing on anything. She was shivering. Austin put his arm around her and she flinched, but slowly she came back into the present.

She turned to him. 'I had a terrible dream,' she whispered.

Austin pulled her closer. 'Don't worry,' he said, 'it's alright. It was just a dream. You're here with me, safe.'

'It was so real, so haunting. A voice, tender but threatening. Loving but sinister. A voice I recognise, somebody familiar. But no images, just a voice in the dark.'

Austin held her tight, gently rocking her. 'It's okay, there's no need to be scared. I'm here.'

They suffered a restless night, Austin attempting to calm Kayla, who kept waking and sobbing. Eventually, morning came and Austin took up his normal duty of preparing coffee and toast while Kayla showered and dressed.

Kayla once again looked at her tired face in the bathroom mirror. 'Girl, you look terrible,' she said to herself.

Within seconds the mist appeared once more in the mirror and started to form the same face as the previous day. The room became colder and Kayla shivered. Without thinking, she touched the face in the mirror and ice formed around her fingertips.

'You're imagining this,' Kayla started to mumble to herself. 'None of this is real. You're just tired.'

The ice started to spread across the mirror and at the same time up Kayla's finger. She watched as the ice crystals reached her knuckle. They were beautiful, sparkling like diamonds, growing up and out like a flower in spring. The ice kept on spreading, growing across the back and the palm of her hand and up to her wrist. She looked back at the mirror and saw a different face smiling back at her. It was as if the person were there with her, so clear was the image. She knew that face, had seen it before, but she didn't know where. A man's face, smiling, almost a grin of satisfaction, of knowing that he was winning at something. Kayla screamed and then fainted.

'Kay? Kay, it's Austin. Can you hear me, sweetheart?'

Kayla opened her eyes and let out a low groan.

'What happened?' she asked.

'I don't know, babe. I was making coffee, heard you scream and sprinted in to find you on the floor. What the hell happened?'

Then she remembered. The cold, the ice, the face. 'Has it gone?' she asked.

'What?' was Austin's reply.

'The ice, the face in the mirror, has it gone?'

She looked at her hand, twisting it in front of her face, examining the fingers, flexing and stretching them.

'What are you on about, babe?' Austin asked.

Kayla stood up and looked in the mirror. Nothing. Nothing except for a small crack in the mirror where her finger had made contact with the glass.

'It's gone,' she whispered. 'Gone.'

She turned and walked back into the bedroom where she examined the mirrors on the doors of her built-in wardrobe. They were perfectly normal. Nothing happened. No swirling mist, no change in temperature, no face.

'Why the bathroom mirror?' she wondered.

'Look, Kay, you're tired. You're working too bloody hard. It's stressing you out.'

She looked at Austin in the wardrobe mirror. He was looking back, an anxious expression on his face. 'Of course, I'm working hard,' she said defensively. 'It's my first year with Kellar and Townsend. They're one of the country's top law firms, who took me on straight after graduation. This has nothing to do with me being tired.'

'Fine,' replied Austin, 'just take it easy, okay? You're not a machine. Now, tell me what happened.'

Kayla took a deep breath, puffed up her cheeks, then exhaled in a long breath. 'Okay, but you're probably going to think I've lost the plot.'

She told Austin everything that had happened, and he noticed how she occasionally shuddered as she recollected the story.

DAY 3

And now – well, now I get to watch you all the time. And that Austin bloke you insist on living with. You know it won't last; I know it won't last. He's just a thug who pretends to have changed; you're a thing of beauty and refinement, like I am. Well, could be. But you're just not ready to give your heart to me yet. You made that quite clear on Friday, so I just have to watch the charade your life has become. It won't be long until I get the courage, the strength, to reach out to you.

Dark gave way to light, and Kayla's mobile phone alarm signalled the start of another day that would include a nine-hour stretch of learning the finer points of law. She awoke feeling refreshed, though, after an incident-free night of deep sleep. Austin completed his usual routine of stretching and head shaking before turning to Kayla.

'How can you look so great in the morning?' he asked.

She didn't really believe the compliment held any truth, but accepted it with good grace. 'Just lucky I guess.'

'Sleep well?' Austin asked.

'Like a baby,' she replied.

Austin grinned. Kayla knew what was coming. 'What, you mean you—'

Kayla cut him off, a finger pointing toward him as a warning.

'No vomit or faeces jokes thanks, Austin. They're not funny, and never have been.'

'Hey, hold on girl, not even a little bit? The boys used to love that gag. Cracked them up every time.'

'Yes, but I'm not one of the lads.'

'You got that right,' Austin replied, a lascivious look in his eye.

Kayla picked up on the look before proclaiming, 'Not a chance. I have to get to work.' She rummaged in her make-up bag, checking she had everything she needed for the day, before glancing up at him and adding, 'But who knows? Maybe later?' She stopped her rummage and frowned. 'Strange, I can't find my compact. Oh well, it'll be around somewhere. Anyway, what are you up to today?' she asked, changing the subject.

Austin replied, 'Young offenders. Doing a talk about how I managed to get out of gang culture and turn my life around.'

'That's brilliant. I'm so proud of you.'

'Hey, it's mostly down to you. You bring out the best in people, you know?' He stood and went to leave the room. 'I'll get the coffee going.'

But before he got to the door, Kayla said, 'I had a strange dream in the night. Not scary, like the last couple of nights, just strange. It was about when we were out on Friday night.'

'Oh yeah? What happened in the replay?'

'Remember that guy who started chatting me up?'

Austin's grin flattened out into a more serious look. 'Yeah, I remember. Works at your place, doesn't he?'

'He said he does, but I can't place him. Anyway, he was in the dream.'

'And what happened?' Austin asked.

Kayla smiled. 'You're not jealous are you, Austin?'

'Nah, course not,' he replied.

'Big, tough gang member like you—'

'*Ex*-gang member,' he interjected.

'Sorry, yes, ex-gang member,' she corrected herself. 'Nothing happened. It played out exactly like it did on Friday, with one difference.'

'What?' asked Austin.

'Well, he didn't have a face.'

'Weird,' was all Austin could respond with before leaving the room.

Kayla enjoyed a longer than usual shower. The hot water felt good; she felt good. A good night's sleep after two bad nights. Maybe Austin was right; maybe she was working too hard. The small bathroom was filling with water vapour, so she switched the shower off and stepped from the cubicle. She wrapped a towel around herself and opened the window to let the steam out. When the mist had lifted she noticed the mirror. The crack had grown longer and was turning on itself, creating a V shape. She surmised that water vapour getting into the crack was causing it to grow. As the steam started to clear, she saw a message written in the condensation on the mirror. She smiled as she read it. *I love you, Kayla.*

Kayla dried herself and walked back into the bedroom where Austin was waiting for his turn in the shower. As Kayla passed him, she brushed his cheek with her hand and tenderly kissed him. 'Thank you,' she said, 'for the sweet message. You're a big softy at heart.'

Austin looked back at her, confusion creasing his brow. 'You're welcome?' he asked more than stated.

Kayla picked up on his confusion. 'The message,' she said, 'on the bathroom mirror.'

Austin smiled, as if the non-existent memory of writing it was coming back to him.

'You're welcome,' he said as he walked into the bathroom.

Closing the door behind him, he turned on the shower. He gazed at the mirror and watched the message appear. *I love you, Kayla.*

'What the fuck?' he said out loud to himself. He rubbed the mirror clean of condensation, but the writing was still there. He rubbed the letter 'I' with his finger. It didn't change, not even a smear. Austin realised the writing was on the inside of the glass.

He started to sweat, started to panic. 'What the fuck is going on here?'

Without warning, the light dimmed, the temperature dropped and a face appeared in the mirror. It was a pale face with red demonic eyes and a mouth that grinned and sneered before announcing, 'Leave her.' The voice was low and threatening. Austin took an involuntary step back and tripped on the base of the shower. He fell back, cracking his head on the tiled wall.

Kayla heard the commotion and ran into the room. The mirror was clear.

'Are you okay, Austin? What happened?' she asked.

'I'm fine,' he replied. 'Just slipped.' He took a quick glance at the now clean mirror. 'Nothing to worry about.' He noticed how cold the bathroom had become. 'Is the heating playing up?' he asked. 'Seems cold in here.'

* * *

It had been a long day at work for Kayla. When she finally arrived home at eight-fifteen she went straight

169

along the hallway into the kitchen, dumped her handbag on a worktop and headed for the fridge while attempting to remove a shoe. She threw the shoe across the room toward the door she'd entered through, simultaneously opening the fridge door and removing a bottle of Prosecco. Slamming the fridge door shut, she removed the other shoe while walking toward a wall-mounted cupboard to get a glass. The second shoe landed with a thud near to the first.

Bath, book, bed, she thought as she headed back along the hallway, turning into the main bathroom, completely missing the note Austin had left which simply stated, 'Had to go out, sorry.'

Kayla relaxed. The stress seemed to leave her like steam leaving a kettle. The wine causing her mind to drift as the day's hardships were lifted from her being.

She was rudely awoken by the splash of her book hitting the surface of the tepid bathwater. A tut later and after fishing the soggy tome from the depths of the bathwater, she climbed from the tub and wrapped herself in a soft cotton towel. Looking in the mirror above the washbasin, she noticed the lines around her eyes. The bags, the luggage delivered by lack of sleep. She was pleased, though, that there was no strange behaviour in this mirror. No smoke, steam or faces, just her own tired reflection.

Her thoughts were interrupted by the now familiar sound of her cat wailing. *Will those two ever get on?* she thought. She left the bathroom, heading across the hallway to the bedroom. Nothing could prepare her for what she saw there. Austin was kneeling on the floor holding Ferdinand in outstretched arms. The cat's body was limp. Austin's hands were covered in blood, which dripped onto the bedroom carpet. A sharp reflective object was sticking out of the cat's body.

'Austin? What happened? What have you done?'

'I've only just got in, Kay. I found him like this. It's a shard from the mirror, from where that crack had grown.'

Kayla's knees weakened when she was hit by the realisation that her beloved feline companion wasn't moving.

'Is he...?' she began to ask.

Austin simply nodded.

Kayla wiped a tear from her eye as shock subsided and anger surfaced. 'What have you done to him, you bastard?'

'Kay, what are you talking about. I've only just got in. You were in the bath. I—'

'Liar! You've never liked Ferd. Always threatening to kill him.'

'Babe, they were just jokes. I love Ferd. Calm down.'

'Don't tell me to calm down. I am calm. You've got form, after all, nicked for carrying. Heading for a—'

'That's unfair. I was being threatened. I carried it for my own protection. No charges were made.'

He gently placed the dead cat on the floor beside him and covered the corpse with a nearby towel. He gestured to Kayla, arms open. 'Come here,' he said.

She could take no more. The tears were now streaming down her face. She rushed at Austin, rage etched onto her face. He managed to catch her as she ran, her arms flailing, pounding his chest. He grabbed her arms and stopped the attack.

While they were engaged in their own little war, they failed to notice the figure forming from the smoke in the wardrobe mirror behind them or the sudden drop in temperature.

Kayla was losing momentum, her attack slowing. Austin wrapped his arms around her, shushing, but this had the opposite effect from what he was hoping.

She pushed herself away, screaming, 'Get your hands off me!' She pushed him hard in the chest and he took a step back, his motion stopped by the wardrobe. The moment he touched the mirrored surface, ice formed on the glass. The room became colder still.

A hand shot out from the glass. Ice forming on it as it extended from the wardrobe door. Kayla's screams of pain and personal loss turned to screams of terror.

'Austin, what's happening?' she shouted.

She watched as a second icy arm emerged from the mirror and wrapped itself around Austin's waist. He was trapped. The mist in the mirror started spiralling around his head in ever decreasing circles before disappearing behind him.

'Kay, help me!' Austin managed to mutter through gritted teeth and short breaths. Kayla was stunned motionless, not believing what she was seeing. In the mirror from behind Austin's head, a shape started to move. It leaned out over Austin's shoulder. A head, smoky and wispy in its form, red-eyed with a maniacal grin. It laughed and pulled Austin. With a gasp and a scream, Austin was taken from the real world and appeared in the mirror. Kayla let out another scream as she rushed toward the mirror. She placed her palm on the cold surface and ice began to form on it. Taking a step back, she managed to remove her hand before it became stuck fast to the mirror with the ice. She looked on, unable to help. The gaseous form of the mirror demon was huge compared to Austin, although Austin appeared to have a solid form, not made of smoke and mist. They both seemed to be floating. There was no visible floor, walls or ceiling.

To Kayla's surprise, Austin squared up to the being in the mirror. He was lean and powerful, nimble, a street brawler. He took a swing at the huge thing in front of him, only for his fist and arm to pass through the eddying mist, connecting with nothing but thin air. The smoke-being laughed, then took hold of Austin's head in one hand. Long wispy fingers wrapped around Austin's skull as he was lifted from a floor that Kayla couldn't see.

'Smash the mirror, Kay,' Austin managed to say as his skull was slowly crushed.

'I can't, Austin, you'll be—'

'Just do it, Kayla! You can't help me.'

The smoky face turned to Kayla, its grin widening, its grip on Austin's skull tightening. With a sickening crack, Austin's skull shattered. Blood and brain matter hit the inside of the mirror with a wet splat. No sooner had the gore made contact with the surface, than the mirror froze over again and then almost immediately cleared to reveal two huge, red, smoky eyes filling almost the entire surface.

'Come to me, Kayla,' a raspy voice demanded.

'Not a fucking chance!' Kayla declared as she grabbed a lamp from her bedside table, hurling it at the mirror. The mirror shattered into a dozen pieces, falling to the bedroom floor.

Kayla stood motionless for a moment, waiting for a sign, for anything to tell her the nightmare was over. She started to cry and sat on the bed, head in hands. Tiredness eventually got the better of her and she fell into a deep sleep. On the floor, a pair of red, smoky eyes tried to find her from the largest part of the broken mirror.

DAY 4

Kayla was filled with dread when she finally woke up. Had it really happened? Was it all just a dream? She sat up in bed and looked at the wardrobe doors, devoid of their mirrors, broken glass on the floor. She started to cry again.

You need to sort this out, Kayla, she thought, *phone work, pull a sickie, clear this mess up.*

She picked up her phone, took a deep breath and phoned her manager. Once her excuse was made, she hung up and sighed, looking once more at the mirror fragments littering the floor. *Okay, let's clear this up.*

She went to the kitchen to retrieve a bin bag and a dustpan and brush. On her return to the bedroom, she switched on the radio as a distraction from what she was doing. The news had just started. One report caught her attention.

'Police were called to a flat in Walthamstow tonight after neighbouring residents complained of a smell coming from the property. Upon gaining entry, the police discovered the body of a man who'd taken his own life by severing the arteries in his left forearm, using what appeared to be a shard of a compact make-up mirror.

'Paramedics at the scene said there was little chance he could have survived the injury and were shocked at how he managed to cut himself so deeply from the inside of the elbow to the wrist, stating that most people would pass out long before reaching the wrist.

'Also at the scene, officers found a book of satanic verses, which contained a slip of paper with the name "Kayla" written on it, apparently bookmarking a single verse.

'The victim is thought to be twenty-four-year-old Kieron Peterson, a maintenance engineer for renowned London law firm Keller and Townsend.'

Kayla promptly switched the radio off, shaken by what she had just heard. A piece of broken mirror caught her attention. Smoke billowed in the shard, before a pair of red eyes formed on the surface. No longer scared, Kayla once again went to the kitchen, this time returning with an empty biscuit tin, a roll of parcel tape and a pair of food tongs. Using the tongs, she carefully lifted the piece of mirror and placed it in the biscuit tin, putting the lid back on once the mirror was inside. She secured the lid by wrapping parcel tape around the tin until it was almost completely covered.

A few minutes later, Kayla knelt on the soft grass in her small garden. She dug a hole and placed the biscuit tin into it, then covered it with soil and patted it down.

'Enjoy the view, you bastard.'

DRUM LESSONS

Mary Camarillo

Neil stacks the lunch plates in the kitchen sink and goes back to the living room. "I'll wash them later," he says as he sits down in the recliner next to Stephanie's. Their chairs are identical except for the color of the afghans folded neatly over the back of each, hers lavender, his forest green. She'd crocheted both of them years ago before her arthritis got bad.

Stephanie smiles. "It's all right. I wish I wasn't so useless."

"I'm the one who can't figure out how to load the dishwasher."

"Did you leave some food out for Ringo?"

"I will." He wouldn't. The cat disappeared more than two weeks ago, and he's already washed out the food bowl and put it away. She'd named the grey tabby Ringo as a joke, knowing he didn't care for the Beatles. Although he doesn't like cats much either, he's sorry Ringo's gone, sorry for Stephanie anyway. He elevates his feet to the exact same angle as hers and they watch another rerun of *Behind the Music*, a dumb show they like to make fun of, although occasionally they recognize someone they know in the background, an engineer or a session player or a photographer.

VH1 has never done an episode on Neil's band, Electric Magic, although their story certainly fits the show's criteria for cliché and melodrama. Their lead singer smashed his Corvette into the center divider of the Santa Ana Freeway the day after the band signed a record contract. The label dropped them, and they broke up. No one Neil toured with after Electric Magic recorded anything VH1 would be interested in. It was all a long time ago.

"You want some ice cream?" he asks during a commercial. Stephanie doesn't answer, so he assumes she's asleep. He must have dozed off too because an episode about Bon Jovi is on when he wakes. They both hate Bon Jovi.

"I'll find something else," he says. Stephanie's head is facing him now, her eyes wide open and bluer than ever before. "What's wrong?" He reaches for her hand. It's cool to his touch and his heart misses a few beats. He lowers his chair and gets up, knees locking at first and then creaking into movement. "Wake up, sweetie." He squeezes her forearm gently. She's always been a pale woman who bruises easily and needs to be careful in the sun, but now her skin has a bluish tint. He shakes her a little and her head slumps down on her neck at an uncomfortable angle.

"Oh Jesus, Stephanie. Are you dead?"

All these months he's done his best to take care of her and now he's let her slip away, alone. She'd been looking right at him with some wonderful last words to share, and he'd been snoring in his recliner like the old man he is.

He turns off the television, centers her head, closes her eyes, and picks up the cell phone from the table in between them.

The phone is a model designed specifically for seniors with a big screen and large buttons, pre-programmed with his daughter's and son's numbers. He hesitates, tapping a three-over-two-pattern on the phone's hard plastic case, his go-to rhythm whenever he can't think. "I'll have a better chance of getting Grace," he tells Stephanie, "but she always overreacts. Charlie will be calmer, but he never answers his phone." He's about to call Charlie when he notices the smell of shit and urine. He sets the phone down. He certainly isn't going to let anyone find Stephanie in a dirty diaper.

He gets a sheet out of the linen closet, spreads it out on the carpet, intending to lift her out of her chair and lay her out flat. She hardly weighs anything. He'll give her a sponge bath, change her clothes, and sit her back in her chair. He tries to raise her and his lower back muscles clinch together in a sudden spasm and he has to let go. He stands and takes a few deep breaths. He thinks of himself as reasonably fit for seventy-five, but he doesn't have strength in his arms anymore, not like when he drummed for a living and hauled equipment in and out of vans before and after each show. He'll have to leave her where she is. The chair is leather, though, and she won't like him getting it wet.

He rolls her arms and legs to one side, tucks the sheet under her, and rolls her back again. It takes him five trips around the chair to get her body centered, her head flopping from side to side as he moves her arms and legs. He's crying so hard he can't see and bumps his knee hard into the hinge of the chair. Suddenly there is blood on the carpet, which he assumes is hers until he looks down at his leg. He's ripped a gash across his calf. He goes to get a Band-Aid and doesn't recognize the old man in the bathroom mirror. He can't remember the last time he shaved. He retrieves Stephanie's shower gel from the tub and brings a towel back to the living room. Her pretty head isn't quite straight on her neck, and he's somehow given her a grimace, probably from all the flopping around. He'll have to fix that later. He sees the trail of blood when he goes out to the garage to fill a bucket with warm water from the utility sink. He can guess what Stephanie's thinking. The stains won't come out if he doesn't take care of them right away.

Crying again, or maybe he's never stopped, he undresses her and then gets down on his knees and crawls around her chair, soaping and rinsing her body. Her tight little nipples still remind him of cherries; and despite the grey pubic hair and fleshy tummy, crisscrossed with scars from childbearing and appendicitis and the surgery he'd insisted on that didn't work, he can still see the twenty-two-year-old beauty he'd stolen away from an opening act's bass player all those years ago. He lifts one of her shapely legs and washes between the other. She's always liked the touch of his fingertips.

"You're giving me goosebumps," she'd say. "Don't stop."

"I won't," he says now. He towels her off and repeats the back and forth around the recliner to remove the sheet, apologizing each time her head twists or her arm falls awkwardly. He hates to leave her alone again, but he's forgotten to bring clean clothes, and it takes too long to decide what she should wear. He loves her in the purple paisley dress, but it isn't something she normally wears around the house, and the most important thing right now, he decides, is for everything to look normal. Her nightgown would be easy to slip over her head, but it's tattered and stained. Even though Stephanie isn't a vain woman, she won't want anyone seeing her in that. He finally decides on a newer pair of black sweats and a Springsteen T-shirt from a concert at the Sports Arena last year. They'd gone with Grace and her husband, stood and swayed together to "Dancing in the Dark." He was never a big Springsteen fan, but it was nice of Grace to make the effort.

After he gets Stephanie dressed he wads up the diaper and her soiled clothes in the damp sheet and takes it all outside to the trashcan. It's so bright and hot outside he can't see. Something scuttles across the cinder block wall. "Who's there?" He squints into the sun at a ragged grey cat stretching out his front legs on the wall. Stephanie's cat had almost the same coloring, but Ringo wore a collar with his name on it and was fat and fluffy and didn't have a huge gash across his eye like this scrawny creature.

"Scram," he says, and the cat jumps down into the hydrangea bushes in the next-door neighbor's yard and disappears. Neil goes back to the living room. He doesn't tell Stephanie about the cat because she'll expect him to try and rescue it and he's just too tired. He hasn't slept well for weeks.

"I'll rest a little while," he says. "I'm right here if you need anything."

* * *

It's already getting dark when he opens his eyes. "You hungry?" he asks, and then he remembers and cries for a long time. When he manages to get out of his chair and turn on the light Stephanie is slumped awkwardly to one side but otherwise appears to be sleeping. He thinks about what he should do next. What he should have already done. Call the children. He looks at the clock. Almost seven. Grace will be getting off the freeway from work about now, pulling into her driveway, thinking about what to feed her husband for dinner. Charlie will be heading off to his night-school accounting classes. Seven o'clock also means *The Rockford Files* are starting. Stephanie loves James Garner.

"I'll call the kids later."

* * *

In his younger years Neil was a night owl, but these days he's up with the sun. He heads to the bathroom and takes a long and satisfying piss, something he's not always able to accomplish, which makes this a good start to the day. He brews coffee and heats water for oatmeal. When he finishes he rinses out his bowl and cup and sets them in the sink, frowning at yesterday's lunch dishes. He could have sworn he washed them last night. He goes out to the garage and opens the door. Another hot August morning.

The garage is vehicle-free now except for the bright red three-wheeled bicycle Charlie brought over as a kind of peace offering after Grace sold Neil's Karmann Ghia and notified the DMV to cancel his license. Although Neil refused to ride the trike at first as a matter of pride, now he takes it all over the neighborhood, up to the market for groceries, over to the pharmacy for Stephanie's meds, down to the library to rent DVDs. He likes cruising the streets, tapping on the handlebars, slapping sixteenth notes on the bell. He nods at the housewives out walking their dogs and flirts with the nannies strolling babies. He rolls the trike down the driveway, checks the tires and swings one leg carefully over the seat.

Two streets down and around a corner, young Josh is out in his front yard digging out grass with a hoe. His mother's idea is to get rid of the lawn. Neil isn't sure this is a good plan. Josh's mother has been slightly off kilter since the husband left. She and Grace were friends in high school and just like Grace she works long hours, which means Josh is home alone all day. Neil spends most afternoons giving the boy drum lessons. Josh is a fast learner, reminding Neil of himself at that age. Even the way he holds his sticks, traditional style, elbows in, lips closed, none of that open-mouthed flailing about.

"I finally got that bolero thing down," Josh says. "That classical stuff is cool. I mean, it's not Zeppelin, but it cooks."

"It'll make even more sense once you learn how to read music."

Josh laughs. "I just need to watch more videos."

Neil shakes his head. "We didn't have videos when I started. I can't count how many record players I wore out, playing tracks over and over again."

"What's a record player?" Josh grins. "Seriously, Neil. John Bonham was a genius."

"Ginger Baker was the genius. John Bonham was a maniac. I'm glad to see you're wearing gloves. You need to protect your hands."

Josh wipes his face. "My mom made spaghetti last night. She saved some for you guys. Just a sec and I'll go get it."

"That's nice of her. Stephanie loves your mom's spaghetti."

Stephanie. Dear God. Stephanie. His heart drops down to his prostrate and he makes a U-turn in Josh's driveway.

"Where you going?" Josh asks. "Don't you want the spaghetti?"

Neil pedals home as fast as he can. The scrawny cat is sitting on the front porch when he opens the garage door. "Go away," he yells as he rolls in his trike. He hurries to the living room. Stephanie's jaw seems a little more rigid when he kisses her cheek and she doesn't smell as fresh as before.

"What is wrong with me? I should have turned on the air conditioning." He lowers the thermostat as far as it will go and races around the house, shutting all the windows, closing the blinds. When his cell phone rings he has to run down the stairs to answer it.

"How's Mom?" Grace asks.

He's out of breath. *She looks peaceful* is what he's decided on when his heartbeat slows enough to speak, but Grace interrupts.

"What did you say?" She sounds angry and Neil panics. "Hold on, Dad. I already told you we're not accepting that bid. Get the rep back on the phone and I'll talk to him."

She isn't talking to him. "Honey," he says, "there's something I need to tell you," but Grace still isn't listening. Grace is at work. Her job is important and stressful and makes her short-tempered most of the time. She gets irritated when she has to repeat herself, insists he needs hearing aids. Stephanie is better at smoothing out her edges.

"I have to do every single thing around here. Call me if anything changes."

"Everything has changed."

"I know. It's hard. I'll call you later."

She hangs up. He stares at the phone for a while and then calls Charlie, gets his voicemail of course. Charlie is out in the field, inspecting something. "Son," he says after the beep. "It's your dad. I need you to call me when you can."

He hangs up and looks over at Stephanie. "Now we wait," he says. "Unless you have a better idea." She doesn't seem to, so they spend the rest of the morning watching cooking shows until he realizes it's time for lunch. He opens a carton of yogurt and eats in front of the kitchen window, expecting to see the grey cat, but the backyard is empty and the grass needs cutting. It's too hot and he doesn't have a lawnmower anymore. Charlie will come by this weekend if he doesn't forget. It's time for Josh's lesson anyway. Stephanie worries about Josh being alone all day. "A boy needs a man in his life," she says. "And it's good for you to get out of the house and out of my hair."

"I'll be back soon," he tells her.

This is the hottest summer ever, he thinks as he takes off on his trike. He can't shake the uncomfortable feeling he's forgotten something, a feeling he has too often these days. He's going to play drums, he knows that much at least. He hopes his kit is set up at the venue by now, wherever that might be, his suit hanging in the dressing room. He feels for the set list and realizes his shirt doesn't even have a pocket.

He's confused. There are no more gigs or suits or late nights or set lists. He doesn't even own a kit anymore; he sold it years ago when Stephanie convinced him it was time to quit. She didn't like being home alone at night, especially when the children were small. When his brother-in-law offered a desk job at his trucking company Neil told himself he was lucky he didn't have to wear a tie to work or cut his hair.

At least his trike appears to be on auto-pilot. He pulls up in front of a somewhat familiar house and knocks on the door, recognizes the boy who lets him in and leads him upstairs. The boy sits down behind a drum kit and they work through the practice charts Neil now recalls laying out at the beginning of summer, whenever that was. Warmup on the snare, single strokes, doubles, paradiddles, double stroke rolls. Neil glances up when the kid is in the middle of a rim shot. A pretty woman has materialized in the doorway.

"That sounds good!" She's a little too old to be the boy's girlfriend. Maybe a roommate. Neil tries to stand, but his feet are asleep.

"How's Stephanie?" the woman asks. "Does she have to go far for her chemo?"

"Oh, she's done with that." It's troubling how strangers know things about him and his wife.

"Well," – the woman looks confused – "that's wonderful. Tell her hello for me. You forgot to take the spaghetti." She holds up a container. He knows who this is now. The boy's mother.

"Want to hear a joke Neil told me?" the boy asks.

She gives Neil an anxious look. Neil's worried too. He can't remember telling the boy a joke.

"How do you make a million dollars as a musician?" the boy asks. He doesn't wait for their answer. "Start with two million. Get it?"

"That's too true to be funny," Neil says. "I'd better go."

* * *

The house is freezing and smells like rotting fruit. The message light blinks on the cell phone. Grace's voice, exasperated. "Charlie said you called him. Is everything okay? I don't know why we bought him that phone. He never answers it. He doesn't even know who I am half the time."

"She doesn't mean that," he tells Stephanie. Grace is convinced he's got dementia and the two of them shouldn't live alone. They have good days and bad days like everyone else. Grace will understand when she gets to be their age.

His daughter sounds anxious in her next message. "Dad, where are you? I'm supposed to go out of town for a meeting tomorrow, but I'll cancel it if you need me to. Call me back."

Neil sits down next to Stephanie. "Must be an important meeting if she has to go out of town." He notices the DVD on top of the television. Something about a hotel with marigolds. "That movie's due back Saturday. We might as well watch it now."

* * *

The movie credits are rolling when Neil hears someone knocking at the front door. He opens his eyes and fumbles for the remote, changes the channel to VH1 where an episode about Deep Purple is starting. He glances over at Stephanie.

The grey cat is sitting in her lap, licking her hand. He sits up so fast the blood rushes out of his heart. "Get out of here!" What kind of nightmare is this? That cat was outside, the last he remembers. "Scat!" The cat ignores him. It's chewing on something, a dead bird? Neil jerks to his feet and flails his arms, looking for something to throw. The cat blinks his eyes, licks his pink tongue across his teeth, and Neil can see now there is no dead bird. The cat is eating Stephanie's hand. "Get away from her!" He picks up the cell phone and throws it hard, but he misses and the plastic case slams into the brick of the fireplace and shatters. The cat leaps gracefully from Stephanie's lap and struts up the stairs, stopping at the landing to clean his claws with his teeth.

Whoever is knocking hasn't stopped. Neil peeks out the front window and sees the boy standing there, grinning, holding a skate board under his arm. He closes the drape quickly. What a fool he is. Now the boy knows he's home. He hurries over to Stephanie's recliner. There are bite marks on both hands and her right palm has been chewed down to the bone. Neil feels as if he might vomit. He pulls the afghan over Stephanie's hand and leans over to pick up the pieces of the phone, so dizzy he's afraid he might pass out. The boy is still knocking. Get rid of him, he decides, and he crams the pieces of the phone in his pants pocket. As he hurries to open the front door, the cat charges down the stairs, streaks in between his legs and nearly knocks him off his feet.

"Whoa!" the boy says as the demon disappears into the night. "What's wrong with Ringo?"

"That's not Ringo," Neil says, trying to recover his balance and block the view of the living room at the same time. He can't let anyone see Stephanie like she is.

"Guess what?" The boy smells so strongly of soap and deodorant that Neil's eyes water. "I have an audition tomorrow." He leans in past Neil and waves his hand. "Hey, Miss Stephanie." When did this boy get so tall and what is his name again? "Jeez, Neil. It's cold in there. You got the AC cranked up too high."

"She likes it cool."

"What are you guys watching?" Before Neil can stop him, the boy is inside, walking towards the television set where Deep Purple's classic guitar riff is just starting, the infamous chord intro that every garage band knows how to play. "It's that 'Smoke on the Water' song, right?" He glances over at Stephanie and frowns. "Is she okay?"

"She's sleeping. We should go outside and talk." Neil stares at the boy, willing him not to look at Stephanie again. "Come on." He opens the front door. "Tell me about this audition."

Mercifully, the boy follows. Neil closes the door behind them. He can still feel the bass chords from the song vibrating in his chest.

"You sure she's okay?"

"She's tired. Nothing for you to worry about. What kind of a band?"

"You smell something? Like a skunk?"

Neil keeps his eyes fixed on the boy's face, hoping his own expression looks somewhat normal, and suddenly remembers his name. Josh. "That's coming from Rainbow Disposal. The ocean breeze blows the stench straight down my street. I've already complained to the city council. What time's the audition?" His right arm trembles and he leans against the side of the house to support himself.

"Tomorrow afternoon. It's rockabilly."

"That should be a piece of cake for you. It's pretty much all snare and brushes. Train beats. Stuff you already know. Good luck to you." Neil puts his hand on the door knob.

"Maybe you could come a little earlier tomorrow, help me practice a few things?" Josh flips his skateboard down on the walkway.

"I'll try." Go on home now, he thinks. Josh steps on the board and balances, rolls a few inches forward and then back again. Why doesn't he leave? Neil can hear his heart pounding.

"There must be a dead animal in the bushes or something. You should call someone."

"I will."

"You sure you're okay?"

He isn't going to be able to stand up much longer. "I said I was fine." He turns around and goes inside, slams the door behind him and locks the deadbolt. It's rude, but it can't be helped. Hopefully Josh isn't racing home to tell his mother about Stephanie. The music is oppressive. Surely Deep Purple had other songs besides this monstrosity. He mutes the sound on the television and lights all of Stephanie's favorite candles, tuberose, ylang ylang, cookie dough. He's shaking from the cold, so he goes to the bedroom and pulls on three pairs of socks, two flannel shirts and sweats over his shorts. The house smells like a funeral parlor. He finds an old bandana to tie around his face. Stephanie wants her ashes sprinkled out in Modjeska Canyon under an oak tree he isn't sure he can find anymore. So many things he can't remember and so many things left to do. Clean up the blood. Shave and shower. Bandage Stephanie's hand. Plan how to explain all of it to Grace and Charlie. He takes a few deep breaths.

His pulse is just starting to slow when the sliding door to the backyard shudders violently. Good God! Has Josh's mother already called the police? Or maybe it's an earthquake, or someone trying to break in. He hurries to the back door and pulls the blinds. The grey cat hangs by its claws halfway up the screen, his eyes wild and hungry.

"Get away from here," Neil screams, backing away from the door. He closes the blinds, and tells himself to calm down. The door is locked; he and Stephanie are safe. There's nothing to be afraid of. As he heads back to the living room, he catches a glimpse of himself in the hall mirror, wild eyes above the bandana over his face, and despite everything, he has to laugh. He looks ridiculous, like some maniac cowboy. He should apologize to Stephanie about her hand and breaking the phone and making a mess of everything, but he doesn't know where to begin. It could have been worse, he supposes. At least it's only her hand.

"You ever wish you'd stayed with that bass player?" he asks instead. "Things might have worked out better for you." He holds his breath. He hopes she knows he's kidding.

He's not surprised when he hears someone knocking on the front door the next morning and then Grace's voice. "Dad, it's me. Unlock the deadbolt." He gets up and looks out the front window. Grace's car is in the driveway. Josh stands next to his mother on the sidewalk and immediately stares down at the ground when he sees Neil.

"Let me in, Dad." Grace steps back from the door, holding the scrawny grey cat in her arms, wearing her office clothes.

She'll get cat hair all over her suit and be late to work. The boy's mother will be late for her job too. Josh's color is bad. He looks like he hasn't slept a wink. His fault, all of it. He hobbles over to Stephanie, tucks the afghan securely over her hand.

"You ready?" he asks. She doesn't answer. She almost looks like she's smiling, which he'll take as forgiveness. He opens the front door.

THE SACRIFRICE

A. H. Sargeant

Henry knew there would have to be sacrifices. However, it would be worth it. After all, houses like Fern Cottage did not come on the market every day, or every year for that matter. Resting in the quiet hinterland of Sunbury-on-Sea, it was perfect for him now that he had retired. The former owners, a retired couple, had lived there for only a few months when the husband had vanished one weekend and was never seen again. His wife (or widow perhaps) had struggled with the situation for a year or so but had eventually decided on a closure of sorts, sold up and gone to live with her daughter. As Henry said, it was an ill wind that blew nobody any good.

Henry had been a widower for over five years, and the little country cottage with half an acre of garden for him to pursue his hobby of growing roses, and someone from the village to take care of the housework two or three times a week, seemed to him to be paradise. And so it proved to be. Of course, he realised that it would be some time, years even, before he was an accepted member of the community that was the village of Nether Sunbury.

Perhaps the development of the nearby seaside town had made the villagers more insular, more inward-looking than would normally be the case, but Henry was prepared for this. As it was, Old Jake the postman had for a few weeks past acknowledged his 'good morning' and Mrs Lawrence who 'did' for him had dropped the air of indifference that was her norm and became quite friendly on occasions. All in all, after some six months or so, Henry felt he was well on the way to being less of a comer-in and more acceptable, if not an accepted member of the community.

* * *

Now, there was one event in the life of the village that Henry believed would put the seal of approval on his arrival, the Nether Sunbury Annual Flower Show. Henry's great passion was for rose growing and the soil around Nether Sunbury seemed to bring out the best in that particular plant. Almost everybody in the village grew flowers of one sort or another, but the Rose Society grew roses to perfection. However, Henry's own horticultural talent was also not inconsiderable, and he felt that a good showing at the annual event would firmly establish him as someone who really belonged in the village and perhaps even make him friends from among those who shared his interest in roses.

He knew the Rose Society was something of an exclusive club, but how one became a member, apart presumably from putting up an extra-special showing of roses, Henry couldn't discover. Somewhat surprisingly

(Henry felt) Mrs Lawrence was a member, although she spoke nothing of it and he did not press the point when their conversation touched on the subject one morning. Old Jake too was a member; his roses were the pride of the district, and it was rare indeed to see him on his round without a prize specimen tucked behind his Post Office badge. Matthews, the village butcher, was another. His shop-front in the High Street had specially fitted window boxes that were constantly replenished with blooms from his excellent garden. And there were others. Their combined talents and enthusiasm for floral display, and roses in particular, made Nether Sunbury in the spring, summer and autumn a delight to the eye. Great splashes of colour were everywhere and the air filled with the sweet, sweet fragrance of English blooms in all their beauty and many varieties.

* * *

All this, however, only served to inspire and challenge Henry to reach greater heights himself, and he threw himself into the task of cultivating his roses, ready for the annual show. He had his own methods of course, the result of many years of trial and error in his labour of love, but he also did a little poking and probing, a little amount of horticultural espionage among his neighbours. Not that he learned much from his spying activities, for like Mrs Lawrence they none of them spoke freely about their methods or the secrets of their success. The most he could learn was that some of them relied for fertiliser on a special preparation that included bone meal, but unable to find out more he was left to his own abilities.

And in the event, and at the event, his own abilities did not let him down. His roses had turned out better than he had even dared to hope, especially given this was his first year in a new environment. On the day of the show his roses looked simply flawless.

* * *

The gathering of growers and visitors at the Nether Sunbury Annual Flower Show was very much the social occasion. There were several marquees on the green, one for each of the floral interests represented, plus a few providing for other local activities and serving refreshments. The Rose Marquee (as it was known) had prime position and was by far the grandest, most stylish and sophisticated of them all. As usual, it attracted a great many visitors and, of course, the exclusive membership of the Rose Society was fully in attendance.

The roses exhibited by Henry, to his delight, drew much attention. To his further joy he gained a second place and a special mention as the most promising new exhibitor. It was a very proud and happy day for him.

Towards the end of the day, however, he was a little disappointed to observe that the members of the Rose Society, whose ranks he had particularly wanted to impress, appeared to have departed en masse. He had expected that his success during the day might have opened the door to that assembly, but it hadn't appeared to and he put it down to that peculiar reserve of middle-England and the rural insularity of their way of life.

However, his disappointment was short-lived. It was only a little while later when Henry was thinking about getting ready to leave that coming toward him across the green was Matthews the butcher and the lady who ran the convenience store, both prominent members of the Rose Society. Matthews took him by his arm and the three of them walked backed to the Rose Marquee, which now appeared to have packed up business for the day. As they neared the marquee, Henry noticed with some glee that there was now a 'Closed to the Public' sign at the entrance. He felt sure he was about to be invited to join the most exclusive of clubs.

Once inside, he was surprised to see that the many stalls of roses had been re-arranged since earlier in the day so that the interior of the tent looked a little like a church or a temple. There was even an altar-like table at one end. Henry's surprise turned almost to shock because a figure in white flowing robes kneeling before the table turned out to be none other than Mrs Lawrence! He was further taken aback to see Old Jake the postman – but looking nothing like Old Jake the postman – also robed in white but with a blood-red rose surrounded by a fern motif emblazoned on his chest, wearing a bishop's mitre and carrying a staff. He then saw, with mounting disquiet, several other members of the Rose Society all dressed in the same outlandish fashion. Henry turned to Matthews as if to seek an explanation, only to discover that he too had put on a white robe and, moreover, in his hand he held a meat cleaver!

A strange gasping cry was the only noise Henry could make as several pairs of hands grabbed him and carried him bodily to the altar. He was laid spread-eagled between the decorations of rose and fern, and a moment later Matthews' cleaver had all but severed his head from his body. Despite the gore, one of the devotees eagerly collected the blood that flowed from his torn neck into a bucket obviously prepared and ready for the purpose.

In his final moments, Henry realised that the more proficient rose growers of Nether Sudbury had to make certain sacrifices if they were to continue to be so successful.

AUTHOR BIOGRAPHIES

These are printed in alphabetical order by contributor surname.

Nico Bell

Nico Bell was born in New York in 1983. She started her writing career as a Christian fiction writer under a different name, receiving acclaim for her work in contests run by American Christian Fiction Writers and Romance Writers of America. Her love of psychological thrillers and twisted plots, though, led her to become a self-styled 'purveyor of the weird'. Her dark fiction now appears in several anthologies. She is also a book and movie reviewer for scifiandscary.com and hosts her own weekly podcast called Box Office Refund.

William Quincy Belle

William Quincy Belle says he is just a guy. Nobody famous; nobody rich; just some guy who likes to periodically add his two cents worth with the hope, accounting for inflation, that $0.02 is not over-evaluating his contribution. He claims that at the heart of the writing process is some sort of (psychotic) urge to put it down on paper and likes to recite the following which so far he hasn't been able to attribute to anyone: 'A writer is an egomaniac with low self-esteem.' You will find Mr Belle's unbridled stream of consciousness floating around in cyberspace.

Mary Camarillo

Mary Camarillo lives in Huntington Beach, California with her husband and terrorist cat, Riley. She is currently working on a novel and a collection of short stories. Her stories have appeared in *Extracts: A Daily Dose of Lit*, *Lunch Ticket* and *The Ear*.

Philip Charter

Philip Charter is a writer and English teacher who lives and works in Pamplona, Spain. He is tall, enjoys travel and runs the imaginatively named website 'Tall Travels'. His fiction has been published in *STORGY, Fabula, Argentea, Carillon* and *The Fiction Pool* magazines among others. His piece 'Raft' won the 2018 WOW Festival flash fiction competition.

Joanie Chevalier

Joanie Chevalier is an author, content editor and the founder of Joanie Chevalier Author Services, offering various services for indie authors. She is also the co-founder of *The RAC* (Reader/Author Connection) *Magazine*, a magazine that promotes and encourages the reader/author connection, and founder of the Our Indie Author Room Facebook group, a place where writers in all stages of their career can go to learn, inspire and teach.

Joanie loves the outdoors and nature, reading and editing, and she thinks her two Chihuahuas are adorable. Her writing is a blend of everything she likes to read: suspense, horror, crime, psychological thrillers, non-fiction and good short stories.

Phillip Drake

Even as a young child, Phillip Drake was always conjuring up stories, filling them with colourful characters and sharing them with anyone and everyone who would listen. Since then, he has progressed to longer, more complex works and sharing them with a wider audience. He is the author of several books including *To Be a Saint*, chronicling his avid fanship of Southampton Football Club, and *Dark Window*, a collection of horror short stories.

Sue Eaton

As a girl growing up in Northamptonshire, Sue Eaton became fascinated by the work of authors such as Ray Bradbury, John Wyndham and Terry Nation, developing a lifelong love for a well-written psychological horror story. She worked for many years as a teacher of children with autism. Her writing is now one of her major passions. She has had her work broadcast on BBC Radio 4 and her debut novel, *The Woman Who Was Not His Wife*, was published by Corona Books in 2018.

Ian Gough

Ian Gough started writing in 2016. It took him a while to pluck up the courage. But since deciding to let his imagination dance (or trip awkwardly) across the page, he's already published three books: *Tricks or Treats*, a collection of chilling short stories, *Lotan the Librarian* and *Vladimir Scond, Private Investigator*, the first two books in his fantasy/comedy Core Lands series, set in a world inhabited by many weird and wonderful beings, mystical creatures, kings, queens, heroes and a couple of door-to-door salesmen. He plans to follow these with more stories in both the fantasy and horror genres.

Tina Grehm

Tina Grehm is currently working on her BA in Creative Writing and has won the Roy F. Powell award for short fiction. She spends most of her time with her cats, watching, reading or playing anything with a solid story. She considers herself an exorcist of sorts, purging the voices in her head by putting pen to paper.

T.R. Hitchman

T.R. Hitchman's first crush was on Christopher Lee. She grew up in love with the eerie stories of Edgar Allan Poe and, as a child of the eighties, was profoundly affected by being allowed to stay up late to watch *Hammer House of Horror* on TV. She has written for The Gothic Society and her debut story collection, *Child of Winter – Ten Dark and Twisted Tales*, was recently published by Corona Books.

Simon Lee-Price

Before he moved into academia, Simon Lee-Price was a fiction editor at Virgin Books, where he had the opportunity to work with some great horror authors including Thomas Ligotti and Ramsey Campbell. He turned his hand to writing 'strange fiction' several years ago and has had short stories published in *Interpreter's House*, *Torrid Literature Journal*, *Five:2:One*, *Sein und Werden*, *Sirens Call* and *Breakroom Stories*, amongst others. His short story 'Mophead' appears in the horror anthology *Restless*.

A.H. Sargeant

A.H. Sargeant describes himself as 'an ancient hack, well past his sell-by date', who in a former life was an advertising copywriter, but whose work never leapt off the page into mainstream literature like that of Fay Weldon or Salman Rushdie. He later worked in marketing and in his middle-years was an aviator. Long-since retired, he has returned to his first love of writing, mainly short stories, which he considers an art-form to be cherished.

Mark A. Smart

Mark A. Smart is a software developer by day and a writer by night. He published his first novel, *Don't Reply*, in 2015, an action thriller set in London and Hampshire. His interest in horror can be traced back to the lasting impression his reading James Herbert as a teenager left on him. In his free time these days he enjoys reading, gaming and cycling, and was once a Karate champion. He lives in Leicester with his wife, Charlotte, and two children, Oliver and Emilia.

Suzan St Maur

Suzan St Maur is the founder of the award-winning website resource HowToWriteBetter.net and is a bestselling writer of non-fiction in fields including writing for business and wedding planning. She also works extensively in the third sector, running and contributing to charities in cancer survivorship. In her lighter moments, she also writes joke books, and her volume of humorous and fairly-sweary poems, *Mischieverse*, was recently published by Corona Books.

Horace Torys

Horace Torys is originally from the Midwest in the U.S. He has travelled extensively and lived abroad before settling in New England, which, he notes, seems to have worked so well for Stephen King. He lives there with his wife and three children, and the family's pet tarantula Raz (short for Razputin, the main character of *Psychonauts*). He has recently launched his own YouTube channel, which you can find by searching for his name on YouTube.com.

Wondra Vanian

Wondra Vanian grew up in Eaton Rapids, Michigan, but moved to the UK when she was twenty. She now calls Pontywaun, Wales home, where she lives with her husband and their two chinchillas, three dachshunds and an evil cat. Graduating with a degree in English Language and Literature from the Open University whilst working full-time, she now writes full-time. As well as in her own books *Pale Is the New Tan* and *A Long Time Dead*, her work has been published in numerous anthologies. She has an avid interest in the horror genre and watches a horror movie almost every night, but sleeps with the lights on.

AUTHOR BIOGRAPHIES

Dänna Wilberg

Dänna Wilberg has written, produced and directed multiple award-winning short films, and has produced and hosted TV programmes in Sacramento for over a decade. She is the author of the romantic-suspense trilogy of books *The Red Chair*, *The Grey Door* and *The Black Dress*. Her current work in progress, the paranormal-suspense *Borrowed Time*, is planned to be the first in a new series of books. Aside from writing, Dänna loves her children, grand-babies, 'killer' cheesecake and Karaoke.

Lewis Williams

Lewis Williams is the editor of this volume and founder of Corona Books UK. His literary endeavours have been multifarious, including the insane project of writing a filthy limerick for every town in the UK which didn't already have one to call its own; the results of which were published as *The Great British Limerick Book*. He has two degrees in philosophy (which number might be considered two too many) and worked for a number of years in a number of different roles for Oxford University before his ignominious departure from its employ.

Author Websites and Twitter Accounts

Those authors who have Twitter accounts and/or their own websites are listed below.

Nico Bell
@nicobellfiction
nicobellfiction.com

William Quincy Belle
@wqbelle
williamquincybelle.com

Mary Camarillo
marycamarillo.com

Philip Charter
@dogbomb3
talltravelling.blogspot.com

Joanie Chevalier
@JoanieChevalier
joaniechevalier.com

Phillip Drake
@pdrakeofficial
phildrakeauthor.wixsite.com/website

Sue Eaton
@SueJayEaton
susanjeaton.com

Ian Gough
@LotanB1

Tina Grehm
@TGrehm
tinagrehm.com

T.R. Hitchman
@TRHitchman
trhitchman.com

Simon Lee-Price	@SimonLeePrice
Mark A. Smart	@Mark_A_Smart
Suzan St Maur	@SuzanStMaur howtowritebetter.net
Horace Torys	@HoraceTorys horacetorys.weebly.com
Wondra Vanian	@witchybelle4u2 wondravanian.com
Dänna Wilberg	@DannaWilberg dannawilberg.com
Lewis Williams	lewiswilliams.com

Innovative, brilliant and quirky

Corona Books UK is an independent publishing company, newly established in 2015. We aim to publish the brilliant, innovative and quirky, regardless of genre. That said, we do have a fondness for sci-fi and horror!

A selection of our titles follows on the next pages. For the latest on other titles published by us and forthcoming attractions, please visit our website and follow us on Twitter

www.coronabooks.com

@CoronaBooksUK

The Corona Book of Horror Stories

edited by Lewis Williams

includes stories by William Quincy Belle, Joanie Chevalier, Sue Eaton, T.R. Hitchman, A.H. Sargeant, Suzan St Maur, Mark A. Smart, Wondra Vanian and 8 others

The Corona Book of Horror Stories brings you 16 dark tales celebrating the best in new horror writing.

Herein you will find the brilliant products of dark imaginations, *certainly*; and something to scare you, revolt you or unnerve you, *probably* – it depends on how jaded and degenerate a soul you are. What we can promise you is a wealth of new writing talent with a variety of different takes on horror, the graphic, the sinister, the natural and the supernatural. There's the tale of the breakfast that is life-changing (and not in a good way), the story of the loner whose obsession in life is keeping parasites, a nuclear warhead that lands on the English city of Leicester, cosmetic surgery taken to the extreme of whole body transplants, and more among the many dark delights to be found inside.

Child of Winter

T.R. Hitchman

An old woman harbours a painful secret and meets a young man with a dark secret of his own; a narcissistic journalist learns that the camera can tell the truth in more ways than one; and a boy discovers horrors he never imagined when he set out to get in with the cool kids...

Ten stories of love, loss and disappointment with a dark twist are the product of the imagination of writer T.R. Hitchman, the new master of modern macabre.

The Corona Book of Science Fiction

The best in new sci-fi short stories

edited by Max Bantleman

includes stories by Sue Eaton, Philip Charter
and 14 others

A sampler of the work of the best new writers of science fiction out there? A sci-fi selection box with a mix of hard (science) and soft (science) centres covering the spectrum of sub-genres? A brilliant anthology you'll find hard to put down? A must read for every sci-fi fan?

All these things? We like to think so, and certainly with *The Corona Book of Science Fiction* we've tried to create something special – a multi-author sci-fi collection where each contribution embodies both great imagination and great storytelling, and which collectively covers a mix of themes from the fantastic to the topical, from AI to Z, all topped off with a last story so touching it has been proved to reduce grown men to tears.

CORONA
BOOKS

The Woman Who Was Not His Wife

Sue Eaton

"You hear of people going missing all the time. They just seem to vanish from the world. You wonder if someone has killed them. You wonder where they are."

Brangwen Roberts is one such person. One minute she is playing with her baby daughter in the garden of her home; the next she finds herself in an alien world. But it is not the world of an advanced and enlightened alien race. Technologically advanced alien slave traders have simply sold her on to a planet where the technology and attitudes are more akin to those of Earth's Middle Ages. At first utterly alone, Brangwen needs to summon all her courage and strength of character to survive in a world where greed and intolerance thrive unchecked. Then there's the man who may or may not want her for all the wrong reasons, a journey across strange lands, her only friends a pair of semi-android fellow slaves... and yet, through it all, the different world she finds herself in is in some ways all too familiar to our own.

Sue Eaton's debut novel is not just great storytelling in science fiction but a stunningly original and engaging book that creates a world that will make you think about your own.

CPSIA information can be obtained
at www.ICGtesting.com
Printed in the USA
BVHW071211050421
604207BV00007B/720